Peter Corris was born in the Wimmera in 1942, educated in Melbourne and Canberra, and worked his way slowly north to New South Wales where he has lived since 1976. In Sydney he has been on the dole, worked as a sports journalist, and was literary editor of the *National Times*.

Peter has been a full-time professional writer since 1982. He is married to the writer Jean Bedford and they have three daughters. He divides his time between Glebe and Coledale on the Illawarra coast. His recreations are reading, writing, movies and sport, including learning to play golf.

Also by Peter Corris in Pan:
Set Up
Cross Off

PETER CORRIS

GET EVEN

PAN
AUSTRALIA

First published in 1994 in Pan by Pan Macmillan Publishers Australia
a division of Pan Macmillan Australia Pty Limited
63-71 Balfour Street, Chippendale, Sydney

National Library of Australia
cataloguing-in-publication data:

Corris, Peter, 1942– .
Get even.
ISBN 0 330 27478 3.
I. Title.
A823.3

Typeset in 10/12 pt Aster by Post Typesetters
Printed in Australia by McPherson's Printing Group

This is fiction. No persons or events depicted are factual.

Thanks to Jean Bedford and Linda Funnell for absolutely essential editorial help, and to Jon Lane for providing the title.

For
Geoff and Phil

PART I

1

Burton, the man from the Witness Protection Unit, was already seated at the table when the other two men entered through different doors. He said, 'David Scanlon, this is Luke Dunlop. He'll be looking after you.'

'Dunlop my arse,' Scanlon said. 'You're Frank Carter. You were a patrol man in Five Dock when I was a D there.'

'Gidday, Dave,' Dunlop said. 'A few things have changed since then, haven't they? You going to shake?'

Scanlon, a burly six-footer who towered over the stocky Dunlop, cracked a grin. He was fair, balding and weatherbeaten from hundreds of hours on the harbour at the helm of his yacht. His face and hands were sprinkled with scabby skin cancers. 'Of course I'll shake. You never fucked me over, not that I remember.'

The two men, both ex-police officers, shook hands and sat at the table. At fifty, Scanlon was the older by twelve years. He had attained the rank of Detective Inspector before a series of allegations, internal police investigations and, finally, criminal charges,

1

had caused his resignation from the force. Acquitted of murdering two witnesses in a major Federal police drug prosecution, he had twice been wounded when shots had been fired at his house and his car. His beach house at Bundeena had been destroyed in a blaze that had almost claimed the lives of his wife and teenage daughter. Following that, Scanlon had secretly volunteered to give evidence to the State Counter Corruption Authority's inquiry into links between stock market manipulation and financial journalism.

The meeting was taking place around a table in one of the Redfern offices occupied by the National Bureau of Criminal Investigation, of which the Witness Protection Unit was a part. Dunlop, formerly Carter, had assumed a new identity when he joined the WPU, as many of its officers were required to do. He had been intrigued by the Scanlon job when it was offered to him. After several years of guarding whistle-blowers, criminals granted immunity in return for testimony, disgruntled conspirators and frightened drug couriers, Scanlon represented a challenge and an opportunity. Not only was he a former policeman, almost a colleague, but he had a wife and daughter to be first protected and then guided through the complex processes of identity-assignment and relocation.

Dunlop, childless and divorced, had no particular interest in family matters, but the nature of the case meant that a female WPU officer would be assigned to it. He had taken steps to see that this person would be Madeline Hardy, with whom he had trained and had a brief affair. Dunlop, tiring of the routine in his work and grown sceptical about its value, now believed firmly in mixing business with pleasure.

'Right,' Burton said, observing the guarded, measured contact between the two men. 'I'll leave you to get on with it. David has three or four SCCA appearances to make as you know, Luke. Round the clock stuff until that's done, then we talk about relocation and the rest of it.'

'Somewhere I can sail my ketch,' Scanlon said. He lit a cigarette, although there was a No Smoking notice on the back of the door.

Burton frowned. 'It's usual to get a new set of habits to go with the new identity.'

'Fuck that,' Scanlon said.

Burton shrugged and waved away a cloud of smoke that had drifted near him. He put a sheaf of papers in his briefcase, buttoned his jacket and left the room.

'Prick,' Scanlon said. 'Pen-pushing prick. How d'you stand working for a dickhead like that, Frank?'

Dunlop pushed his chair back and came around the table until he was standing next to Scanlon. 'The name's Luke. You'd better remember that, Dave. Got a smoke?'

'Yeah, course. I remember you were a terror for the weed. Thought you mighta gone all clean-fuckin'-lung on us since then.'

Scanlon took a soft-pack of unfiltered Chesterfields from the pocket of his well-cut suit and flicked it in a practised manner so that a cigarette stood up. Dunlop took one cigarette and then the packet and crushed it in his hand. He ground it between his palm and fingers so that the contents were completely destroyed. Scanlon began to rise from his chair, but Dunlop bore down on his shoulder, pinching a nerve and pinning him. With his free hand he

3

snuffed out the cigarette Scanlon had left burning in the ashtray.

'You're quitting, Dave. Or you're changing to a pipe or cigars or one-milligram filters. Those bloody Chesterfields have been a trademark of yours for too long. You don't need to advertise your toughness any more, mate. You're going to drop out of sight.'

Scanlon worked his wide shoulders, getting free of Dunlop's grip. His neck muscles were knotted with tension and Dunlop noted a sour smell coming from his body, the result of too much alcohol, insufficient sleep and poor personal hygiene. 'I suppose you know what you're talking about. You'd better be good at this, Frank, or I'm dead meat.'

'I'm good at it, and the name's Luke. Get that through your thick head.'

Scanlon's fists bunched. 'Look, you smartarse bastard...'

Dunlop kicked the chair out from under Scanlon. The big man sprawled on the floor and Dunlop stood over him. Scanlon's hand moved to where his service pistol would have been kept. Then he remembered that he didn't have a pistol any longer and looked at the hand as if it had suddenly become palsied. Dunlop righted the chair.

'Get up, Dave,' he said. 'I'm just trying to make a point. You've got to learn to control that temper of yours because you're going to run into a lot of situations that'll piss you off. Plus, you're not a copper any more, and soon you won't even be an ex-copper. You're going to find life very different.'

Scanlon got to his feet and brushed off his clothes. He slumped back into the chair and felt for his

4

cigarettes. Dunlop handed him the one he'd taken. 'Lucky last, mate. Enjoy it.'

Scanlon lit the cigarette, expelled smoke and made a visible effort to control his feelings of humiliation and outrage. 'I don't remember you as a hard bastard, F ... Luke.'

'You don't remember me at all. We just met today. Right?'

'If you say so. Tell you the truth you look bloody different. You're a couple of stone lighter, shaved off the moustache and cut your hair different. Is that what I'm going to have to do?'

'If you're smart you will. I can't make you, but you'd be surprised to know how many blokes in your position who end up on a slab looked just the way they used to look. More of the ones who've made the effort to change are still walking around.'

Scanlon nodded and managed another grin. He felt the roll of flesh at his waist. 'Well, it wouldn't do me any harm to get rid of this, but shit, you can't ask me to give up the boats. That's about the only decent thing in my life, apart from my kid.'

Dunlop sat down and poured himself some water from a carafe on the table. *Have to get a grip on myself*, he thought. *That was all rougher than it needed to be.* 'We'll get on to her. Have to do something about those skin cancers, too.'

Scanlon scratched at his right hand. 'Yeah, Lucy's been on my back about that for years. What d'they do, burn them off or something?'

Dunlop shrugged. 'I don't know exactly. Have you ever had a beard, Dave?'

'Fuck, no. Anyway, it's all white now. A beard'd make me look like an old man.'

5

It was Dunlop's turn to smile. 'That's what you want to be, don't you?'

Dunlop had coffee sent in, and over the next three hours the two men talked. Dunlop's purpose was to get from Scanlon the name of every enemy he had ever had, every person, policeman or civilian, who might have a grudge against him. In particular, the people who would be threatened by the evidence he was to give to the SCCA investigation.

'Shit,' Scanlon said at the beginning of the session. 'You want me to recall the name of every crim I've put away, every bastard I've laid a hand on, every whore I've had a freebie off?'

'No, just those who couldn't take it. The ones who threatened you or talked tough about you. You know the ones I mean.'

Scanlon, drinking cup after cup of strong coffee and suffering the pangs of nicotine withdrawal, racked his brains for names and details. Dunlop took notes, thinking that the names, violent stories and unsavoury rumours Scanlon came up with were the warp and weft of a policeman's life. A few years back, his own professional past could have been painted in similar colours. He was glad to be out of it and suspected that Scanlon felt the same. The ex-detective, however, maintained a tough facade, emphasising that he wasn't afraid of the 'cock-roaches', 'animals' and 'scumbags' who had littered his life.

The psychology lectures Dunlop had attended in his training period hadn't made a deep impression on him. He was impatient with notions of the 'insecurity of bullies' and the 'impotence implied by excessive physical and verbal violence'. In many ways, he still operated like a policeman, and he felt it necessary to break down Scanlon's bravado.

'Wouldn't like to go inside with 'em though, eh, Dave? How'd you like a couple of days in the yard at Long Bay with Les Watson?'

'I wouldn't last that long,' Scanlon said. 'Look, that's about all I can give you from the old days. I might've missed a few, but for all I know some of them are inside or fuckin' dead by now.'

'All right. Let's move on to the songs you're going to sing now. Get this straight, I'm not interested in the details of what you're going to say. Understand? I just want the useful names. If you're going to put in the boss of the Stock Exchange, I don't want to hear what you've got on him, just who he'd use to shut you up.'

Scanlon swallowed a mouthful of lukewarm coffee and looked haunted. 'Jesus, that puts you in the driver's seat, doesn't it? What if you're bent and fancy a few shares in this and that? You could sell me for a fuckin' fortune.'

'You're getting the idea, Dave. Trust nobody. But look at it this way—if you don't cooperate, I'll advise the SCCA people that you have no fears for your safety and that routine police protection will suffice.'

Scanlon stared at Dunlop. His ruddy skin had lost colour and lines of tension were deeply etched around his eyes and mouth. 'Jesus Christ, you can do that?'

Dunlop nodded. 'You've been promised immunity, Dave. That's important. I imagine your legal

7

costs are being met and there are negotiations about a relocation compensation package and allowance. Right?'

'Yeah. Right.'

'It's not worth a rat's arse if you're dead or if someone gets to your wife and daughter.'

Scanlon picked at the scabs on his hands. Flakes of skin fell on the polished surface of the table. 'You still married?'

Dunlop shook his head.

'I shouldn't be. God knows why she stuck with me. I gave her a hundred and one fuckin' reasons to leave over the years. You have any kids?'

The bravado had evaporated and Dunlop sensed that he was getting close to the root of Scanlon's character and motivation now. He was disposed to be patient, if not sympathetic. 'No.'

'Mirabelle's sixteen, going on. Terrific kid. Bit wild, the way they are at that age. You've seen 'em. They'll try anything. Take risks. Shit. I just don't think I could bear to see her going down the tubes the way so many kids like her do. That's one of the reasons I'm doing this. They've promised me Fremantle.'

'Sure,' Dunlop said, 'why not?'

'That'd be the place for us. Out of all this shit. Quiet. A bit of land. A four-wheel drive. Horses and boats.'

Not much of that sounded like Dave Scanlon to Dunlop. As a senior detective he had been known for his interest in gambling, women and money. The yachting was the only exception to a set of pursuits that were best carried on indoors and at night. Dunlop made a mental note to find out the details of Scanlon's yachting career. Since it looked like something the client was unwilling to abandon, consideration would have to be given to modifying it in some way.

'Okay,' Dunlop said, staring into the grounds of his last cup of coffee. 'Tell me who's likely to be serious.'

'Loomis, for one.'

Dunlop whistled. Scanlon had named an assistant police commissioner with a reputation for passionate devotion to the police culture. 'You mean on general principles, hating blokes who rat on their mates? Or what?'

'I thought you didn't want the details. Wait till I give you the other name and you'll get some idea of it. Now Walter Loomis has saved the arses of a lot of blokes in the force over the years. Quite a few who'd be willing to do him a favour.'

'Like?'

Not for the first time, Scanlon rubbed his ear, as if clearing an obstruction inside it. Dunlop made a mental note of the habit and poised his pen ready to write.

'You'll love this,' Scanlon said. 'I'd nominate Keith Krabbe, Ian McCausland and Trish Tillotson. You'd be familiar with Ian, wouldn't you? Heard of the others, I suppose.'

Dunlop had. McCausland had been the officer in charge of the Kings Cross station where Dunlop had last served as a police officer. Then Detective Sergeant Frank Carter, he had been accused, with some justification, of taking bribes from pimps and madams. He had, but most of the money had been channelled back into helping the prostitutes get abortions, receive medical treatment, enter detoxification programs. McCausland, Carter's chief accuser, was himself totally corrupt and serving the interests of the vice operators when he had Carter cashiered. Krabbe had killed more men than any other policeman in recent New South Wales history. When the press became aware of his statistics, he was quietly shifted sideways out of operational police work into a senior managerial position.

Dunlop scrawled the names on his pad. 'Trish? I remember the rumours. You sure of your facts?'

'You better believe it. She's the hot-shot queen. I could tell you about, oh, seven, eight ODs she's personally supervised.'

'Is that what you're going to tell the SCCA?'

'Nah. I don't expect so. Might have to. Depends on how it goes. Jeez, I could do with a smoke.'

'We're nearly finished. I get the feeling you're only moderately worried about Loomis and his lot. Am I right, Dave?'

Scanlon went through a series of movements that were almost tics—scratching his scabs, working at his ear and fiddling with his cigarette lighter. Suddenly, he became still and looked across the table at Dunlop. His face was that of a man pushed to the limit. He was summoning all the courage he had to utter words that carried more importance to him than any others he had ever spoken. 'My main evidence is about Thomas Kippax. You knew that?'

Dunlop nodded. 'To do with stock market fiddling and the stuff that gets published in his magazines. Sounds a bit dry to me.'

'That's the word they've let out. Only that shit Burton and one bloke on the SCCA committee know what I've *really* got to say. Christ, I hope I can trust you. I'm putting my life in your hands. That's not so

10

much, I've had a good run, but Mirabelle shouldn't ...'

Dunlop was astonished at the mental agonies Scanlon appeared to be going through. He looked, not like a man who has made his decision, but like one still wrestling with the necessity to decide. In his experience, evidence-givers, whistle-blowers, informers, enjoyed a feeling of relief. They were fearful of the consequences, but drew some comfort from having made the plunge. Not so with Scanlon. Dunlop could tell when a client was about to change his or her mind and attempt to pull back from the agreement. Scanlon showed no signs of being in this state of mind either. Dunlop, expecting a routine case apart from the prospect of linking up again with Madeline Hardy, was interested.

'You know how Kippax puts out all these magazines—*Business Daily, Business Week, Business Monthly*—all that shit?'

'Yeah. I can't say I read them.'

'Remember when he took control of them?'

Dunlop shrugged. 'Few years back, I seem to remember. I've never really kept up with the business news, Dave.'

Scanlon drew in a breath and let it out slowly. From across the table, Dunlop caught again the smell of alcohol, tobacco and poor digestion. 'He got them when his older brother died. I helped to set up the hit.'

11

2

Dunlop found himself forced back in his chair, like an astronaut experiencing a hundred Gs. Scanlon's statement explained everything—the mans' initial aggression and bravado, the tinge of fatalism about his own prospects and the very high level of fear.

'With his money, Kippax could hire anyone,' Dunlop said slowly. 'Foreign talent, say.'

'You bet he could, and he would. Like I'm telling you, he's done it before. It's not something he'd have to stew over. He's got lines open into the police—state and federal—and into some of the intelligence agencies.'

'Jesus, Dave,' Dunlop said. 'You've really stuck your neck out, haven't you?'

Scanlon sniffed, pulled out a handkerchief and wiped his face and eyes. Dunlop was unsure whether he was dealing with a respiratory problem or tears. 'High stakes, mate. They want to nail Loomis, Kippax and quite a few others. It's fucking political, as always. If those big heads roll, other smaller heads stay safe. It's all a lot of crap, this corruption inquiry stuff. Just a matter of passing the buck and protecting the right arses. You must know that.'

Dunlop shrugged. 'I just deal with the operational aspects. I'm a caddy, not a player. D'you play golf, Dave?'

'Now and again.'

'We'll have a round or two,' Dunlop said. 'Somewhere, sometime.'

'What the fuck does that mean?'

'It means you're a challenge to me, mate. I've tucked away quite a few people since I've been in this game. It turned out that nobody cared with some of them. Some of the others, a lot of people cared. But you've got more problems than any other man I ever heard of. Unless you're lying.'

Scanlon picked the longest butt out of the ashtray with his blunt, thick fingers, straightened it and put the end, minimally, in his mouth. Working carefully, with the lighter flame turned low, he got the butt lit and inhaled deeply.

'You'd have got a good bit of lighter gas with that drag,' Dunlop said.

'Get stuffed. What did you mean by that crack about me lying?'

Dunlop shrugged. 'It happens. Blokes in your boat are called clients. We get women too, of course. Well, some clients lie to big-note themselves. They tell us this big-time operator is after them, or that fully paid-up nut case. All to get a higher level of protection and maintenance, see?'

'You'd have to be fucking crazy,' Scanlon said. 'Just to get a whiff of the real stuff'd put you off that game. Jeez, I've...'

Dunlop leaned forward. 'Yes, David? What were you about to say then?'

'You cunt. You put the wind up me then.'

13

'Keeping a little something to yourself, are you? Something to bargain with if the going gets sticky? I've been through it too many times, Dave. I've handled more clients than you've cooked up verbals. No, maybe not. But I know how it looks from your end.'

'Fuck you. How could you?'

Dunlop was silent. He could have told Scanlon about the simulations they had been through in the training course—the real-life, real-threat scenarios that had left some of the trainees failed and hospitalised. He doubted that the former detective would be impressed. Other genuinely hazardous situations—his confrontation with Kerry Loew and the menace represented by Dennis Tate—were not things he could talk about. He watched as Scanlon took a few desperate puffs on the diminishing butt and was glad that he'd given up the weed and was now an 'occasional' rather than a 'social' drinker. Addictions were too revealing of vulnerability and weakness. He sipped some water and projected calm and stillness.

'I'm not fucking lying,' Scanlon said.

'A few more names then. One might do. The blokes you call the pen-pushers might believe Kippax hasn't got an inkling of what you're going to talk about, but I don't. Your nerves are shot, Dave. I know you from the old days. It was always a joke and a wink with Dave Scanlon, even when the dogs were sniffing real hard. You're not joking and winking now.'

Earlier in the session, Scanlon had undone his top shirt button and slid down his loosened tie. Now he restored it, in somewhat bedraggled condition, to its proper position. 'That's it. No more to say.'

14

'You're holding out on me,' Dunlop said angrily. 'I don't advise it. If you reckon you can take care of any of this on your own, you're nuts.'

Scanlon stood. Rising to his full height seemed to give him renewed confidence. 'What's the next move?'

'As of now, you're under our protection. Burton tells me you've hired a few bodyguards.'

Scanlon nodded. 'Just to keep an eye on the house at night and to keep tabs on Lucy and Mirabelle.'

'You'll be able to pay them off. I'd like to get a look at your place. See if it's all right to keep you there for a while. Until you've fronted up for your first session, say. The level of threat to you is highest before you start and after you finish.'

'That figures,' Scanlon said. 'But I think you should get the womenfolk out of the way now.'

'Possibly. Let's go and take a look.'

Dunlop and Scanlon went to the car park under the Redfern building and got into Dunlop's Ford Laser. Scanlon's lip curled a little when he saw the car. 'This is the best they can do for you? Gutless little job, isn't it?'

Dunlop went through his routine of checking the car over thoroughly before unlocking the door. 'I don't have to do a lot of high-speed chasing these days,' he said, as he settled behind the wheel. 'It's the sort of car no-one notices. That's the important thing. What d'you drive? I mean, what *did* you drive?'

'Christ, it's going to be like that, is it? I've got a Merc.'

'Could be worse, depending on the colour. White is it? Grey?'

'Red,' Scanlon grunted, 'with white upholstery.'

'Shit. I suppose you've got plates saying "Davo"?'

'Get fucked.'

Scanlon lived in Randwick. Dunlop knew the address and drove skilfully through the early evening traffic. In mid-November, with daylight saving in operation, Sydney was warm through most of the day, but experienced a cooling wind as the sun sank towards the skyline. Dunlop appeared relaxed, hummed under his breath, but was constantly on the alert for anything unusual—a car pushing up hard from behind or cutting across from another lane. He looked for vehicles that appeared to be travelling in tandem, particularly a truck and a car or a car and a motorcycle. Nothing threatening appeared. Scanlon was tense, particularly when he reached for his cigarettes as he did several times on the drive. Part of Dunlop's task was to keep the client cooperative and, as far as possible, relaxed. It was the aspect of the work he was least good at. Aggressive and inclined to be insensitive to the feelings of others, he tended to communicate those attitudes. He glanced sideways at Scanlon, who was picking at one of his skin cancers.

'So, where do you play golf, Dave?'

'The Cliffs course, behind Prince Edward hospital. Know it?'

'Heard of it. Tricky?'

'Depends on how you play. Lot of water as you'd expect—not a problem if you can give it a whack. Not many bunkers. What's better—your long or short game?'

'Long. Putting's lousy.'

'You'd be all right then. Greens are good. It's getting a bit of distance off the tee that screws up the roughies.'

'Sounds interesting.'

'Yeah, let's have a game. Be a good place to see if anyone's paying me any attention. You can put a few blokes on the course. They'll enjoy the day out. What about tomorrow?'

Dunlop was unused to clients taking the initiative in this way, but he saw some merit in the suggestion. To his surprise, he was beginning to enjoy Scanlon's company. 'I'll think about it.'

Scanlon forced his hand away from his face, patted his pocket for cigarettes again and sighed. 'Of course, I'll have to check it out with her ladyship, Lucy, first.'

Dunlop made the turn into Carrington Road, smiling to himself. Dave Scanlon was one of the last men on earth he'd have expected to be henpecked. The Scanlon house was a sprawling, modern ranch-style building, long and low, set on a big corner block. *Good,* Dunlop thought, *two sides securable.* There was a chest-high brick wall all around surmounted by a metal fence at least as high, providing a formidable barrier. The double gates were set in solid brick pillars and opened by a remote control device which Scanlon now took from his pocket.

'Big spread,' Dunlop said as he drew up at the gates and waited for Scanlon to operate the remote control. 'Must have cost a bit.'

'I earned it.' As Scanlon spoke, a man stepped from a car parked across the street and approached the Laser. Scanlon wound down his window and leaned out. 'It's okay, Geoff. It's me. Where're the girls?'

17

Geoff was a muscular, blond crew-cut specimen in white T-shirt and faded army fatigue pants. His right hand was thrust into a deep pocket, the arm flexed for a quick movement. 'Shopping, Mr Scanlon. Russell's with them.'

'Right.' Scanlon pressed a button on the black box and the gates opened. 'You can park in one of the slots,' he said to Dunlop. 'There's three.'

Dunlop braked halfway up the gravel drive. 'Here'll do me.'

'You'll drip oil on my gravel.'

'Dave, that's going to be the next owner's problem, not yours. Pretend I'm a buyer. Show me around.'

'Funny bastard.' Scanlon got out of the car and groaned as his joints creaked. 'I'm out of condition. I'll have to ride a buggy when we have that round.'

'Not with me you won't,' Dunlop said. 'You'll walk every bloody metre and carry your clubs. Start of the new man you're going to be. We'll have to think of a name, too... What's wrong?'

Scanlon was standing in the middle of the drive, looking towards the back of the house. The fading light bounced off the blue-green surface of the swimming pool thirty metres away. Scanlon loosened his tie again. 'Jeez, I could go a beer. I can't understand where Rusty's got to.'

'Rusty?'

'My dog. Shepherd with a bit of dingo in him. Bloody great watchdog. Rusty!' Scanlon let out a low whistle, but there was no response. 'Rusty, you great bludger! Where are you?'

The two men walked past the three-car garage. The roller doors were open and Dunlop could see

18

the rear end of the red Mercedes and the back wheel of a motor scooter. Scanlon whistled again and clapped his hands but there was no sign of the dog. 'Can't understand it,' he muttered.

Dunlop motioned Scanlon to stop as they reached the breezeway between the garage and the back door of the house. He took out the .45 automatic he carried in a hip holster and checked the action. 'Check the back door, Dave.'

'There's an alarm. Geoff would have heard if anyone had...'

'Just check it!'

Scanlon moved cautiously across to the house and examined the screen and the closed door. Dunlop noted with approval that the big man kept himself pressed close to the wall, out of sight to anyone inside the house. 'Looks all right,' Scanlon said.

'Stay there.' Dunlop moved past the garage to a paved area behind the house. He crossed that and approached the twenty-five metre swimming pool. At the far end there appeared to be a shadow under the low diving board. The shadow lengthened as Dunlop walked beside the rippling water. At the halfway point he realised that what he was seeing was not a shadow, but a stain slowly spreading out from something floating there. He heard Scanlon come up behind him, wheezing from having trotted the short distance.

'Jesus Christ,' Scanlon said. 'It's Rusty.'

3

Scanlon insisted that his wife and daughter should not return to the house. Geoff communicated with Russell by mobile phone and Dunlop used his own mobile to arrange for the two females to be taken to a WPU safe house. He requested that Madeline Hardy be assigned to these clients, the operation being given the code name 'Thoroughbred'. He knew that Maddy Hardy would appreciate the reference—they had first consummated their passion in the Thoroughbred Motel in Randwick, after circling each other for several wary weeks.

Scanlon gave Dunlop his key and instructed him how to switch off the alarm system. Dunlop went into the house, gave it a once-over to make sure it contained no surprises, and brought two cans of beer back to the pool area. Scanlon had hauled the dog out and he squatted beside it, his shirt sleeves and trousers soaked with the stained water. The big dog had been struck very hard on the head several times and then slashed across the throat. The head wound was clean now, showing splintered bone, pink flesh and oozing brain pulp. Scanlon straightened up, wiped his hands on his shirt and accepted the can.

'Mirabelle loved that dog. I couldn't let her see this.'

Dunlop nodded and popped his can. 'How did Rusty feel about strangers?'

Scanlon looked down at the dog. 'He wouldn't savage them, but he'd bark to wake the fuckin' dead and he'd stand them off. Jump about, growl, all that carry-on. I can't see how anyone'd get close enough to do this to him.'

'Have a drink,' Dunlop said. 'Tranquilliser dart'd do it easy. It'd be quiet, too. Knock him out and then do the rest.'

Scanlon opened his can clumsily and took a long pull on it. 'Cunts.'

'This is a warning. This says lay off, shut up. What d'you say, Dave?'

Scanlon flopped down into an aluminium and plastic pool chair. 'I say fuck 'em. Mind you, I haven't got much choice. I'm facing a heap of charges if I don't play along. I've got to tell you I'm not guilty of most of them, but I can be made to *look* guilty real easy. You know what it costs to hire a good QC these days?'

'I can guess.' Dunlop sat and drank some beer.

Scanlon squinted at Dunlop's can of light beer. 'What're you drinking that piss for? I only keep it in the house for Mirabelle.'

Dunlop shrugged and Scanlon went on. 'Yeah, I'd be bankrupt after it went a couple of days in court and completely skint by the time it finished. Plus I might lose. They've got my balls gripped good and tight.'

Dunlop was not sympathetic. Scanlon, he knew, had skated on thin ice as a policeman for many years, taking the kickbacks, playing the odds, risking the falls. He knew how the system worked and

21

shouldn't have been surprised when some of its sharper teeth bit him. But Dunlop's job was not to judge, just to protect and preserve. He enjoyed the sporting element in it and, just occasionally, there was a client who deserved his best services. To stay good at the job, he believed, you had to practise the skills, even though that mostly meant working for the unworthy.

'This is flash stuff,' Dunlop said. 'Killing the dog like this. Serious, but sort of dramatic. What does that suggest to you?'

Scanlon had almost emptied his can in a couple of seconds. He drained it and crumpled it slowly in his big mottled fist. 'Nothing.'

'You're lying, Dave.'

Scanlon shrugged. 'I'm fucking tired is what I am. I was up half the night with...'

'Yes?'

'Never mind. What do we do next?'

'I'd suggest you go and have a lie-down. Geoff can do something about the dog and then he and Russell can take off. I'll get some of our people over. What can you tell me about the neighbours?'

Scanlon did indeed look tired. The dark bags under his eyes sagged down towards his cheeks and a vein in his forehead was throbbing. He shrugged. 'Doctor of some kind over the back. Good security set-up to protect his art collection. Invited me in to have a look at it once. Pile of shit it seemed to me.'

Dunlop jerked his thumb at the high cyclone fence on the side of the block. 'What about there?'

'Tennis court. That's what the fence is for. The odd ball comes over just the same. Rusty used to eat 'em.' Scanlon chuckled and then coughed and wheezed.

'Jeez, I'm going to miss that dog. The bloke there's in advertising. Poofter I think, but it's hard to tell these days. Drives a Porsche.'

'Names?'

'Doctor Farnham, like with that singer. The poofter's name is Dempsey, can you believe it? I checked them out when I moved in here. They're okay.'

'Have a rest,' Dunlop said. 'I'll explain things to Geoff.'

Scanlon heaved himself from the chair and stared at Dunlop. 'You've changed. I used to think you didn't have the gumption to do the job in plain clothes. You were a bit of a bleeding heart as I recall.'

'We all change, Dave. And you're going to have to do a hell of a lot of it.'

Scanlon bent and picked up the jacket he'd dropped by the side of the pool. He looked briefly at the dog and lumbered off towards the house. Dunlop used his phone to summon a security team. He deliberated and then called another number.

'Doctor Carstairs here.'

'Ted, Luke Dunlop. I've got a client—overweight, fifty plus, lot of stress. His colour's bad and he's got this blue vein in his forehead. Looked like it was sort of throbbing.'

'Hmm. Smoker?'

'Yes, but I've told him he'll have to stop.'

'Taper him off, don't cold turkey him. What's he doing now?'

'Lying down.'

'Let him rest. Get him to take a shower and keep an eye on him. The vein's not necessarily a problem. Relax him. A few quiet drinks wouldn't hurt, bit of TV and some exercise. See how he pulls up in forty-eight hours. I take it he's expendable?'

'Isn't everyone? Thanks, Ted.'

'You're welcome.'

Dunlop winced as he cut the call. He hated being told he was welcome and being instructed to have a nice day. He feared Americanisation as much as he disliked the monarchy and everything that went with it. He considered himself a republican, and had been told that the French and German models of how republican constitutions worked should be adopted by Australia. He had problems with that idea, too. It was an uncomfortable stance, but Dunlop had seldom experienced comfort.

He made arrangements with Geoff for the removal of the dog and the termination of his and Russell's services. Geoff was a hireling of a large security services firm and it was no skin off his nose, once Dunlop had shown him his credentials.

The bodyguard drove off with the body of Rusty, wrapped in a tarpaulin, in the boot of his car. Dunlop wandered around the large block, noting the professionally tended garden and high level of maintenance of the house and pool, until his three-man team of minders arrived. He briefed them on the killing of the dog and the likelihood that the perpetrator had entered the property over the back fence. They were experienced and needed little instruction. Dunlop knew that the fence would be watched, that the team would immediately search the house for weapons and drugs, would send out for food if required, maintain contact with him and generally keep Scanlon secure without constraining him too much.

'Grog?' Dieter Weiss, the leader of the team, asked.

'Supply him, but keep it moderate. There's some kind of games room in there—darts, pool table and all that. You blokes might like to take a few bucks off him. Sorry you can't take a dip, unless you fancy swimming in dog blood.'

Weiss grinned. 'What about the neighbours?'

Dunlop ripped a sheet from his notepad. 'Here's the names. You can run them through. The client reckons they're okay, but it wouldn't hurt to check. I'll be at the place in Sans Souci.'

The safe house was at the end of a spit of land running into the Georges River. Two cottages had been joined and extensively renovated to provide a complex of apartments where WPU clients could be housed along with their minders, providing security and a measure of privacy. The half-acre block was surrounded by an electrified fence which a closed-circuit television system monitored inside the building. Tall gums and casuarinas planted around the periphery provided an effective screen from the other houses in the vicinity. At the end of a grassy stretch running from the back of the house to the water was a boat dock where a small motor launch was kept moored.

Dunlop left his car in the street and used a key to unlock a door in what looked like an ordinary brush-wood fence. The accent was on unobtrusiveness, suburban normality. In fact the fence was heavily reinforced and the key defused a sophisticated alarm system and identified its user to the computer that controlled the security functions. He avoided the sprinkler playing in the small front garden and opened a side door with a similar electronic key. The TV cameras would have relayed his picture inside to

25

be checked against his key code in the computer's data bank. Dunlop distrusted the high-tech apparatus, believing that it made the personnel lazy and was likely to fail. He had been told that it was necessary for 'credibility' and had been unable to think of an appropriate rejoinder.

The woman who met him in the narrow hallway was, like him, in her late thirties. Again, like Dunlop, she was of average height and compactly built. Her dark hair was cut in a spiky style; she had slightly heavy features with brown eyes and a wide, generous mouth. She wore a white shirt and tight black ski pants with medium heels.

'Hello, Luke.'

'Maddy.'

She gave a small, throaty laugh. 'Thoroughbred.'

'I thought you'd get it.'

'I wore the pants. Same ones.' She made a slow full turn, mock-coquettish.

'You look great,' Dunlop said. During their brief affair he had admitted to finding ski pants with a strap running under the foot worn with high heels erotic. Madeline Hardy had been amused.

'You look pretty good yourself. A bit greyer.'

Dunlop touched the hair he wore short and carelessly brushed back. He felt awkward seeing Maddy again after almost three years. He'd thought of her often and wondered how far they could take things. From what he remembered they were very alike, but he didn't know whether that was a plus or not.

'You must have a bit of clout these days,' Maddy said. 'Get your own way with things, do you? I was told I was wanted on this and that was it.'

'It's a big one. I guess they'll let me handle it until I

26

cock it up. I wanted you because I know you're good.'

It didn't come out the way he intended. Maddy frowned and turned away. 'You'd better come and meet them, then.'

Dunlop moved forward quickly and put his hand on her shoulder. 'I wanted to see you again as well.'

'Let's see how it goes. First things first. You look a bit worn. Are you drinking these days?'

Dunlop grinned, remembering that Maddy was an enthusiastic and knowledgeable wine drinker. 'D'you call light beer drinking?'

'I call it palate death and a waste of throat muscles. But come on, I'll give you one. You need to relax. You'll freak them, looking all intense like that.'

Bossy as ever, Dunlop thought. But he quite liked it. He followed her down the passage, past several doors, and into a kitchenette, where she opened a bar fridge and took out a can of Tooheys Blue Label and a half-full bottle of white wine. She handed him the can and poured a small amount of wine into a glass.

'Well, what d'you make of them?' Dunlop said.

'The woman's a little kittenish thing. Tough as a brick underneath, I'd say. What've they got in mind for her?'

'Her hubby wants to live the quiet life.'

Maddy sipped her wine and shook her head. 'I can't see it.'

'What about the girl?'

'Stroppy. More open than her mother. Hormone-driven, if you know what I mean.'

'Sounds more like her dad.'

'She's not a bad kid,' Maddy said. 'Wants us to bring her dog over.'

27

4

Thomas Kippax placed his pale, hairless hands on his desk and leaned slightly forward, lizard-like. It was a mannerism of his to swallow after he began speaking. 'So,' he said and swallowed, 'what've we got?'

With the magazine proprietor was Edgar Georges, who held the rank of Chief Inspector in the New South Wales police force, and Detective Sergeant Patricia Tillotson. Georges had often been passed over for promotion to higher rank on account of his addiction to gambling and too-close association with notorious Sydney criminals. However, his connections in the force built up over twenty-five years' service, his involvement in a complex network of favours done and obligations incurred, made it impossible for reformers to displace him. Trish Tillotson was a dark, angular woman in her forties. When she was a junior constable a woman she arrested suggested that Tillotson's darkness was due to Aboriginal ancestry. The report on the arrest Constable Tillotson submitted did not mention this, deposing only that the suspect had become 'violent and abusive' and that it was as a result of the action taken to subdue her that she had lost an eye. Trish Tillotson was feared by male and female police officers and criminals alike.

'Not much, Thomas,' Georges said. He was florid and grossly overweight, filling a commodious chair in Kippax's office suite, and with jowls sitting over his shirt collar. 'They've kept this fucking thing as tight as a transsexual's twat. Excuse me, Trish.'

'I bet you talk about it more than you do it, Edgar,' Tillotson said. 'Don't mind me.'

'I keep hearing rumours.' Kippax said, 'that there's a mystery police witness. Everyone knows about the bastards who used to work here and are going to rat on me. I'm working to minimise the damage there. I think I can contain it, more or less. I was hoping you could tell me something about this colleague of yours.'

Tillotson shrugged. The easy way her square shoulders lifted and dropped suggested that she was fit. 'I've got no proof, but I think it could be Keith Krabbe. He's as pissed off at being put out to graze as Edgar here is about being stuck on the level he's on.'

'Jesus, Trish,' Georges growled, 'you're a hard-nosed bitch. On those grounds it could just as well be me.'

Tillotson's thin mouth relaxed into the semblance of a smile. She turned slightly in her chair, but looked not at Georges but past him, out at the lights of the city visible from the fourth-storey window. 'Anything to say, Edgar?'

'Fuck you.'

'There you go again.'

Kippax was fifty years of age, tall with cropped

grey hair and pinched features. His chin was receding and his neck long. Business-obsessed from his teens, he was an indoors man with a pale skin and an underdeveloped body. His washed-out blue eyes were weak and he wore heavy horn-rimmed spectacles with thick lenses. 'This isn't helpful,' he said. 'I can't see any particular problems with Krabbe.'

Georges chuckled emphysemically. 'Walter Loomis can. Keith was his boy from way back. There's quite a lot Keith could say about this and that.'

'Not without putting himself in the shit,' Tillotson said.

Georges took out a packet of cigarettes but put it away when he saw Kippax frown. 'Could've done some kind of immunity deal with him. You know how it works. You could be in the same boat yourself one day, Trish, with some of the creative policing you've done.'

'I'll be in any boat except one with you. When's your next medical, Edgar? Reckon you'll make it?'

'My dad weighed twenty-two stone, lived to eighty-five.'

'Your poor mother.'

'This is not amusing,' Kippax said severely. 'If Walter Loomis comes under attack, that could be a problem for me. He handled certain delicate tasks and handled them well. Got well rewarded, too. I didn't ask how he did his delegating, of course.'

'If it was really heavy stuff, he would've used Keith for sure,' Georges said. 'If it was more in the way of persuasion, he probably used Ian McCausland. That could work out all right, all round.'

'How so?' Kippax asked.

'Ian's got the big C. Matter of weeks to go, they say.

30

Won't see Christmas. If I was Walter, I'd do a deal with his missus and get Keith to load Ian up with every piece of shit I could. That's if it *is* Keith who's doing the talking.'

Kippax nodded. The jobs Walter Loomis had done for him were persuasive rather than coercive—blackmail of business rivals, charges laid against competitors and later dropped, the planting of false evidence. It would be convenient to blame a dying man, especially if he could be convinced to make certain admissions. He imagined that Walter Loomis would anticipate that angle, too. But he had summoned Georges and Tillotson to probe for another name. One he had heard whispered and which concerned him far more. He spun around in his chair, catching his knee on the edge of the desk—he was a clumsy man—and opened the drinks cabinet and bar fridge behind him. Something of a hypochondriac, Kippax did not normally drink after eight p.m., believing that alcohol in the system at night was damaging, but this was an exception.

'What'll you have?' he said, trying for a friendly, social tone but missing by a wide margin.

Edgar Georges couldn't recall ever being offered a drink by Kippax before. *Bastard must want something*, he thought. 'Bourbon and coke. Thanks, Thomas.'

'Trish?'

'What're you having, Thomas?'

'I thought a little white wine.'

'I'll have the same, thanks.'

Kippax prepared the drinks deftly enough. He had mastered certain skills necessary for business success, if not the manner to go with them. He opened a

31

cigar box on his desk and slid it across towards Georges. 'It's the smell of cigarettes I can't take, Edgar. A good cigar's a different thing altogether.'

Georges took a swig of his drink, finding it satisfactorily strong, and leaned across to take a cigar. He unwrapped it, nipped the end with the attachment on the desk lighter and got it lit. Trish Tillotson sipped her wine and sneered slightly at the cloud of smoke being puffed from Georges' thick, livercoloured lips. 'This is very nice, Thomas, but what's it in aid of?'

Kippax hesitated. He dealt in information and disliked releasing it for anything less than its market rate. But sometimes it was necessary. 'I've wondered for some time about another of your former colleagues—David Rodney Scanlon.'

Georges puffed smoke and shook his head. The flesh wobbled and Trish Tillotson looked away in disgust. 'Dave's finished. Resigned, took a pension. He was never what you'd call a big player anyway, not really.'

Tillotson waved smoke from her face. 'I wouldn't say that.'

Kippax lifted one sandy eyebrow. 'Would you care to comment further?'

'No. Not until I hear what you've got.'

'Suspicions, mostly. Scanlon's name has … come up, shall we say. There was an incident at his house tonight. He has a security guard, by the way.'

'Not surprised,' Georges said. 'House of his got fire-bombed a while back. People don't realise what the police go through. What happened?'

Kippax drank some wine. 'I don't have the details, but my information is that there was a considerable

32

amount of activity afterwards. Some pictures were taken, and this man,' Kippax opened a drawer and took out some blown-up photographs, 'appeared to be in charge of operations. I wonder if either of you know him.'

He slid several of the prints across the desk and Georges and Tillotson reached forward to take them. Georges turned a photograph in his bloated fingers to allow more of the muted lighting in the room to fall on it. His eyesight was poor but, despite his porcine ugliness, he was too vain to wear glasses. He squinted at the face, paled-out by the night photography. 'Looks familiar,' he grunted. 'But I can't put a name to it.'

'I can,' Tillotson said sharply. 'That's Luke Dunlop, a.k.a. Frank Carter.'

'Carter,' Georges muttered. 'I remember him. D at the Cross. He got kicked out for corruption. Doesn't look much like him to me.'

'He's lost weight, Edgar. Like you should. Used to have a gut that hung over his belt and a moustache that hung over his mouth. He's scrubbed up pretty well, but I know him. The girls around the Cross had a lot of time for him.' Tillotson tossed the photograph back on the table and sipped some more of her drink. Her attitude was challenging.

'All right, Trish,' Kippax said. 'Why the revamp and name change? What do you know about him?'

Tillotson emptied her glass, put it on the desk and gave it a slight nudge towards Kippax. The magazine proprietor filled it and topped up his own glass. Georges' glass was empty but Kippax ignored it. 'Before we get to that, Thomas, I think you should tell Edgar and me what's *really* going on.'

Kippax shook his head and a few flakes of dandruff dropped onto the shoulders of his dark jacket. 'I can't do that quite yet. But if what I suspect is true, I'm going to have need of your services. And the rewards will be greater than before.'

Tillotson turned slightly to look very deliberately at Georges. 'I don't know, Thomas. With this SCCA inquiry on you're getting just a little bit warm. The inducements would have to be very good.'

Georges was confused. His liver was in an advanced state of degeneration and it took much less liquor these days than formerly to affect him. He hadn't been exactly sober when he entered the meeting, and the strong drink he'd consumed had pushed him close to insobriety. The cigar was a rich, heady drug as well. It seemed to him that Trish was threatening Kippax. That couldn't be true. Best to say nothing. He clamped his jaws around the Havana and returned Tillotson's gaze uncomprehendingly.

'The inducements will be excellent,' Kippax purred. 'As hitherto—payments into your trusts, stock options.'

'I'm worried about the paper trail,' Tillotson said.

Kippax suppressed his anger, made another drink for Georges and added some wine to his own glass, spilling a drop or two as his hand shook slightly. 'Don't be. I have the best people available working on that sort of thing. It's become an art form and the artists are getting better at it every day.'

Tillotson knew when she had pushed as far as she could. 'All right, Thomas. Dunlop, who was Carter, is WPU. If he's minding Dave Scanlon, you can bet Scanlon's an important witness. It doesn't surprise me. Unlike Edgar, I always thought Dave *was* a player. I take it you had some dealings with him?'

'Not exactly,' Kippax said. 'But thank you, Trish. That's very useful information.'

Georges had consumed half of his second drink and was struggling to stay in touch with the conversation. 'Hard to put any pressure on Dave,' he mumbled. 'Out of the force. Pension and investments. Tough bastard.'

'I might have the answer there,' Kippax said. 'With Trish's help.'

5

Lucy and Mirabelle Scanlon were watching television in a comfortable sitting room towards the rear of the Sans Souci house. The woman appeared to be interested in the program—a Clive James documentary on the fleshpots of Budapest—but her daughter was bored, flipping through a magazine and pointing a remote control at the set, threatening to turn it off. She looked relieved when Dunlop and Maddy entered the room.

'At *last*,' she said. 'Someone who can tell me what the fuck's going on.'

'Just because it's a man,' Lucy Scanlon said, 'doesn't mean you have to use your father's gutter language. It also doesn't mean he's going to tell us any more than she did.'

'Don't give me your feminist bullshit.' Mirabelle stood up and approached Dunlop. She was tall with gingery hair and a fair complexion, like her father, and lean the way he might once have been. She wore jeans and a Guns 'n Roses T-shirt with high-top sneakers. She made a fist and practically brandished it in Dunlop's face. 'You. What are we doing here?'

Dunlop, childless and with very little experience of

36

young people since he left the police force, was disinclined to accept Mirabelle's behaviour. 'I've just left your father,' he said. 'He told me what a good kid you were. Ms Hardy here's just told me the same. They must be talking about someone else.'

The teenager's aggression level dipped immediately. 'You've been with Dad? How is he? Could you *please* tell us what's going on?'

'That's better,' Dunlop said. 'Why don't we all sit down? I imagine you can tape that program if you want to, Mrs Scanlon. My name's Dunlop, by the way.'

Mirabelle snatched up the remote control and switched off the set before flopping back into her chair. Lucy Scanlon's movements were almost languid. She was wearing a silk dress with a floral pattern and a short skirt. Her shoes, with very high heels, were lying on the carpet beside her chair. Automatically, she felt for them with her feet and slipped into them as Dunlop addressed her. She patted her elegantly styled auburn hair, and seemed to arrange her porcelain-doll features to reflect intense interest in the person with whom she was communicating. 'It's quite all right, Mr Dunlop. I was just passing the time.'

'Jesus,' Mirabelle said, cranking up again. 'Easy for you. That's all you ever do.'

Lucy Scanlon ignored her daughter completely. 'I imagine we adults have a good deal to discuss.'

'We do,' Dunlop said. 'But Mirabelle's a part of it.'

'Mirabelle is a child. For the next few years at least, thanks to her father's indulgence, she will continue to think and act as a child. Consequently, she has nothing to contribute to this discussion. What would you say was the subject of this meeting, Mr Dunlop?'

37

Dunlop could not recall the last time he had felt so manipulated. There was something almost mesmerising about the woman's icy calm and certainty that things would fall as she wished. Against his will and better judgement, he said, 'Life and death.'

Mirabelle said, 'Fuck you all,' picked up her magazine and left the room.

Lucy Scanlon sighed and gestured for Maddy and Dunlop to sit down. Dunlop stared at her, unable to reconcile the image of this coiffed, polished creature with the shambling roughness of David Scanlon. He had expected someone strident and tough, perhaps with a veneer of recently acquired sophistication. He had no doubt of the toughness, but he found the rest of her presentation impossible to assess—was it old-money, deportment schooling or play-acting from start to finish? Maddy shot him an amused glance.

'Where is my husband?'

'He's at home.'

'Why are we here?'

Maddy looked again at Dunlop, who seemed helpless to keep from responding like an automaton. 'Your dog was killed and dumped in the swimming pool,' he said. 'Evidently as some kind of warning or threat. We thought it best that you didn't go back to the house.'

'I see. Well, I must say I never cared for that mangy mongrel anyway.'

Maddy's anger made her lean forward in her chair. 'Your daughter asked for the dog to be brought here. What d'you think she's going to say when she finds out it's dead?'

Lucy Scanlon shrugged, barely lifting the lightly

padded shoulders of her stylish dress. 'Her father will come up with some way of softening the blow, as he has with every hard fact she has ever faced.'

Maddy's instinct told her that all Dunlop would get from this self-contained woman would be what she wanted to volunteer. 'Are you aware of your husband's present situation, Mrs Scanlon?' she asked.

The almost imperceptible shrug came again. 'Up to a point. I gather he is going to lay information against some of his former associates in order to protect himself from criminal proceedings. Very sensible, if a little late in the piece.'

'You don't sound very sympathetic towards him, or towards your daughter, if you'll excuse me saying so.'

'I can hardly hope to stop you saying whatever you please in an establishment like this, Ms Hardy. David has ... provided well for me up to this point. Or almost up to now. The last few years have been ... difficult. To be honest, I'm not sure that I can go on ...'

Dunlop's snort of derision made both women start. He was back on his own territory and assertive. 'I don't think you understand anything, Mrs Scanlon. The killing of the dog is sort of ... symbolic. It means you and Mirabelle are targets just as much as Dave. If it means anything to you, Dave's more concerned about that than for his own safety.'

'Bravado. Macho bullshit, as his daughter would say.' Lucy Scanlon rose from her chair as if she was about to sweep out of the room. Then she looked around and saw that there was nowhere to sweep to, and that her companions were unlikely to be

39

impressed. She sat down and crossed her shapely legs. 'Do you think I might have a drink?'

Dunlop picked up on Maddy's slight nod. 'What would you like, Mrs Scanlon?'

'Scotch and ice, please. You must excuse my sharpness. This is all very difficult and I'm on edge.'

'We're every one of us on edge, Mrs Scanlon,' Dunlop said, thinking that this was the first real sign of it she'd given. 'That's what this business is all about. Maddy?'

'Some white wine, please.'

Dunlop went out and Maddy leaned forward in her chair. 'This is hard for you,' she said. 'It's none of your doing, but your husband is in a very dangerous situation and...'

Lucy Scanlon had recovered ninety-nine per cent of her composure. 'I wouldn't say that.'

'Wouldn't say what?'

'That David's difficulties are his responsibility alone. He wasn't overly ambitious, but I could see the opportunities. I pushed him, Ms Hardy. Pushed him quite hard, and for a time it all went quite well. Do you know how disgusting a policeman's job really is?'

Maddy shook her head. 'Not really.'

'Almost no-one does. It's vile, dealing with the dregs of society day after day, week after week. The only other people who get their hands that dirty are saints of various sorts. Bound-for-heaven types. Well, policemen are sinners, and they want some rewards here on earth.'

It was a standard defence of police corruption, but Lucy Scanlon obviously embraced and accepted it powerfully. Maddy nodded non-committally. 'Has

Mr Scanlon told you what you're facing—relocation, changes of identity?'

'My husband doesn't *tell* me things, Ms Hardy. These matters have been discussed.'

'And what is your attitude?'

'Everything is negotiable. Ah, good, thank you so much, Mr Dunlop.'

Dunlop handed glasses to the two women and nursed a coffee mug himself. He was tired and hungry, rattled by Lucy Scanlon's forcefulness and Mirabelle's hostility, and unsure of Maddy's attitude towards him. While he'd been out of the room he had checked on the security and accommodation arrangements. The Scanlons were the only clients in residence. Apart from Maddy there were three other WPU officers, two men and one woman, taking shifts at the TV monitor, manning the phone and fax machine and simulating normal activity around the place. Lucy and her daughter had their own bedrooms adjoining the sitting room where she was presently sipping her drink. They shared a bathroom, an arrangement Dunlop thought unlikely to be workable for long, and had only the clothes they had been wearing when picked up.

Lucy finished her drink quickly, the first hurried movement she had made. She stood and smoothed her dress. Even in her high heels she was diminutive, with a figure that was slightly rounded without being plump. 'I'm rather tired. I think I'll go to bed.'

'There are some toiletries in your bathroom,' Maddy said. 'I could lend you a nightgown.'

'Thank you, but I'd swim in it, my dear. I can sleep in my slip.' The glance at Dunlop was minimal, but sufficient. As intended, he had a fleeting image of

41

that small, efficiently arranged body in a silk petticoat.

'Good night, Mrs Scanlon,' Maddy said.

'Good night to you both. I have to say that I'm quite impressed with your procedures so far. But I must give you fair warning—as of tomorrow I will start to become a little ... demanding. For example, I don't like to spend two days in the same dress.'

Not to mention the shoes and underwear, Maddy thought.

Dunlop said, 'If you could make a list of what you want from the house and leave it out here, I'll see that the things are brought over. Perhaps you could ask Mirabelle to do the same.'

'Thank you. All she ever wears are jeans, T-shirts and sweaters, but I imagine she'll have some specific requirements from her record collection.' Lucy's face looked older as she moved out of the patch of dim light she'd been occupying. There were lines around her eyes and mouth not noticeable before. She smiled suddenly, showing small, even white teeth and a flash of pink tongue. 'It's a pity about the dog. Good night.'

Dunlop and Maddy went back to the kitchenette that adjoined Maddy's room. 'Jee-zus,' Dunlop said. 'I thought I'd seen hard.'

'Come on, Lucas. She got through to you. Going to trot over there tomorrow and pick up her smalls, are you?'

'Thought I'd get you to do it. You might learn a thing or two.'

'Stuff that. You don't look the best. When did you last have a decent meal?'

'A decent meal? I don't remember. I haven't eaten anything since midday. What've you got here? I could knock something up.'

'You never did enter the nineties did you? The fridge is full of stuff to stick in the microwave. You can be eating something hot in ten minutes.'

Dunlop chose lasagna. Maddy put the package in the oven, poured another few inches of wine for herself and opened another light beer. He ate and drank, telling Maddy, between mouthfuls, what he'd learned from Scanlon about the evidence he would present, the enemies he faced and the indications that he had surprises in store for the SCCA. Maddy listened in silence and watched him, thinking that he'd aged more than he should have in the time since she'd last seen him. She knew some of the details of his career, particularly two woundings he had suffered, but nothing of what he'd been through emotionally. The frown lines between his eyebrows had deepened. When he'd finished eating she noticed that he'd developed a habit of gnawing at the inside of his lower lip.

'He's holding back,' Dunlop said. 'It's going to be messy. I can feel it.'

'You can always use the daughter to prise it out of him.'

'Yeah, I thought of that. This is a shitty business, isn't it?'

'They told us that in training. Do you have a normal case load now, or do you just do these big-time jobs?'

'I've got a case load, but these things get priority, and with so many inquiries going on they seem to be coming up more and more. What about you?'

43

She nodded. 'Case load plus bits and pieces. I'm doing a bit of instruction myself these days.'

They chatted about aspects of the job. Maddy did a tour of inspection and when she returned Dunlop put his arms around her.

'Only if you promise it's not in place of fucking either of *them*.'

Dunlop kissed her. 'The job got in the way the first time. I thought I'd get some revenge on the job. I've been thinking about you, Maddy.'

To their surprise, it was as if the intervening years hadn't happened. As lovers they had been immensely compatible, with similar quirks and the same preferences as to position and pace. In her room, on the three-quarter bed, they fell straight back into it. Maddy liked to begin passively, being undressed and caressed and talked to. In some mysterious way this brought her to a point of arousal, close to orgasm, that launched her into assertive, energetic foreplay. They were both muscular and fit, and the love play was close to wrestling, almost a test of strength. They paused for Maddy to roll the condom onto his erection, and when Dunlop pinned and entered her she resisted momentarily and then opened to him, drawing him down and folding herself around him.

'Oh, Jesus,' she moaned. 'Oh, darling. Oh, I love that. I fucking love that!'

Remembering, Dunlop rolled to the side, allowing her to curl up and press against him, getting leverage and finding a rhythm. They fucked energetically, sweating and gripping shoulders and hips. Maddy came first and Dunlop rode in on the last spasms of her orgasm like a surfer following a collapsing wave to the beach.

44

Later, when they had peeled apart, she said, 'God, that was good.'

Dunlop nuzzled at her firm, small breasts. 'It's always so religious with you. Makes it dirtier and more fun.'

'I should go and check on things one more time,' she said. 'The bloody job.'

Dunlop rolled over and hugged a pillow. 'You'll find me asleep, love. But my Dick Tracy wristwatch alarm will wake me in time.'

'For what?'

'You want a real man, don't you?'

'Sure.'

'Davo and me are gonna play a round of golf.'

'Jesus,' Maddy said.

'There you go again.'

6

Dunlop spent most of the morning on the telephone. He rang the Randwick house and asked
about the client's state of health. He was told that
Scanlon had slept well, eaten breakfast and was chip-
ping golf balls on the back lawn. He had organised for
his regular maintenance man to clean the pool. Dunlop arranged for Lucy Scanlon's and her daughter's
clothes to be collected. He rang Burton and others in
the WPU to discuss the intricacies of the case.

Peters, one of Dunlop's superiors, said, 'Did he tell
you something it would be inadvisable for us to talk
about on the phone?'

'Yes.'

'Good, I thought he might. That's some confirma-
tion. We can't be sure it's the truth. What's your
judgement?'

'Hard to say. He's a shrewd, experienced man.
Truth isn't something hard and fast with him.'

'Point taken. How're things down there by the
water?'

'Tense and bound to get tenser. We're going to
have to come up with something else, especially for
the wife. You can feel her costing the furniture.'

'Like that? We're working on it. I take it Ms Hardy can keep the lid on things for a day or two?'

'Not longer.'

'Well, the ante goes up when he opens his mouth. We'll have the press to worry about, more lawyers than you can shake a stick at, phone tappers—the lot. Stay with it, Luke.'

Dunlop phoned Scanlon and agreed on a tee-off time. Then he spoke again to the team, arranging for officers to be present on the golf course. As he put the phone down he became aware of Mirabelle, smoking a cigarette, drinking a can of Coke and leaning against the door jamb. He could see that she was regarding his crumpled clothes and unshaven face thoughtfully.

'How's Dad?' she said.

'He's okay. Want to come over and see him? We're playing golf this afternoon.'

'Golf, yuk.'

'You could caddy.'

She laughed, then scowled as if annoyed with herself for being amused. 'No way. If you were sailing it'd be different.'

'Another time then.'

Mirabelle blew smoke, shrugged and slouched away. Dunlop reflected that her manners were excessively bad in the same way that her mother's were excessively good. Psychology territory. So far, all exchanges with Maddy had been cool and professional as the safe house personnel busied themselves with their various tasks. Before he left he took her aside.

'Everything okay?'

'Lady Muck's giving me a bit of a hard time. She's

hard to like. The kid can't decide which one of us to shit on most. Otherwise, not too bad.'

'They're working on another venue. You'll be the first to know.'

'Put 'em in orbit for a year, I say. What about the dog dilemma? Who breaks the news?'

'Shit, I forgot.'

'Don't worry. I'll do it. Take care, Luke.'

Dunlop drove to his house in Marrickville, showered, shaved, ate a sandwich and collected his golf clubs. Stopped at a slow light on the drive to the eastern suburbs, he flicked open his *Guide to the Golf Courses of Sydney*. He learned that the Cliffs course had been the brainchild of some golfing doctors in the 1940s. Originally a nine-hole layout, it had been extended to eighteen when more land became available in the 1960s after the closing of the old quarantine station. 'A links course, par 71, 5486 metres for members, with undulating fairways, dominated by the ocean and water. Several stretches of water to hit over, few bunkers.' On the whole, Dunlop preferred bunkers to water.

At two p.m. he conferred with the man in charge of the protection team, a nuggetty Lebanese named Sammy Tadros.

'It's not bad,' Tadros said. 'The hospital's secure and you've got the sea on that side. A man placed up there with field glasses,' he pointed to a high point near the middle of the course, 'can keep a pretty good eye on things.'

'Good,' Dunlop said.

'Course, you're fuckin' mad to be out here hitting

48

little balls around in the sun. Doesn't the man play pool?'

'*I* don't play pool,' Dunlop said. 'The man needs to relax, get some exercise, develop confidence in the people looking after him. If he sits around at home all day doing nothing, who knows what useless thoughts might run through his head?'

'So you're going to let him win, are you, Luke?'

'If I have to.'

Scanlon arrived with two WPU officers. He unloaded a newish set of Ping clubs and an aluminium buggy from the boot of the car and wheeled the kit across to where Dunlop stood with his bag. It was Wednesday and the course was almost deserted in the warm afternoon. Scanlon's grin was wide as he shook hands with Dunlop.

'Wednesday's quiet,' he said. 'The fucking doctors're busy carving people up and the members are buggered after a Stableford comp and a piss-up they have on Tuesday. I had a word with the pro on the blower. We'll be right.'

'What did you tell him?'

'That I wanted to have a quiet round with a villain and that we'd be having a bet or two. I said there'd be a couple of hundred in it for him. You'd be able to handle that, *Luke*, wouldn't you?'

Dunlop laughed. 'You're a bastard, Dave. Starting to suck on the tit straight off, eh?'

Scanlon pulled out a wood, slipped off the cover and began to take practice swings, apparently untroubled by the dangers facing him. Dunlop watched the fluid motion, unimpeded by the man's bulk. The competitive instinct in him was strong and he said, 'Your wife and daughter are all right.'

49

More well-grooved swings. 'I know.'

'How's that?'

'Mirabelle rang me just before I left home. Let's get on with it. While I'm feeling loose. Ten bucks a hole?'

'You're on,' Dunlop said, still mulling over the communication between Scanlon and his daughter. He wondered what else, if anything, had passed between them other than affirmations of well-being. Maybe Maddy would know.

The first hole was a longish par four with a ditch and some ti-tree scrub running up the left side of the fairway. There was a rough patch about two hundred metres out where the ground dipped. A decent right-tending drive and a straight, medium iron shot should see the ball on the slightly elevated green. A light breeze was blowing into the players' faces. They tossed for first strike and Dunlop won. Confident of his driving, he hit the ball straight down the fairway and was astonished to see it land far shorter than he'd expected.

'Wind's tricky here,' Scanlon said. 'Have to keep under it.' He took a one iron and hit his ball low and right, finishing fifty metres past Dunlop's and better positioned for the next shot. Dunlop over-clubbed and put his ball in a bunker at the back of the green. Scanlon's five iron ended two metres from the pin. Dunlop's trap shot left him about the same distance away. Both men took two putts to get down and the hole was Scanlon's.

Dunlop was carrying his clubs while Scanlon was wheeling his lightweight buggy. As they progressed to the second tee, Dunlop noticed a man strolling along in the rough, apparently looking for lost balls.

He recognised him. 'I need a caddy who knows the course,' Dunlop said. 'You out-foxed me there, Dave.'

'Part of the game,' Scanlon said.

Dunlop won the next hole and exposed a weakness in Scanlon's game. Both men hit seven irons onto the green, but both were left with ten-metre putts. Dunlop put his close, but Scanlon's ball, missing the hole by only a few centimetres, went well past. Dunlop tapped in but Scanlon took two more putts to hole out.

'You gave that a whack,' Dunlop said.

'I hate to squib a putt. I'd rather have a go than come up short.'

The new few holes were halved at par or bogey with both playing steadily and staying out of trouble. On the long, par four, eighth hole Dunlop's drive carried beyond a fairway bunker 250 metres out and skipped off a hard mound to land a hundred metres from the green.

'Shit,' Scanlon said. 'You're a lucky fucker.' His drive landed in the bunker. Dunlop birdied the hole while Scanlon made bogey. In an odd way, Dunlop found that observing the security precautions around the course helped his game. He noted the flash of field-glasses in the far distance; the man repairing divots on the sixth fairway was WPU and he was sure the groundsman fiddling with the sprinklers around the seventh green was familiar. The golf course was a series of valleys and plateaus and by the ninth hole Scanlon was showing signs of weariness. Dunlop, twelve years younger and a four day a week jogger, was feeling no strain. He observed Scanlon closely as the big man hauled his

51

buggy up the rise to the tee. He was sweating and short of breath but not actually distressed. Unlike Dunlop, who had smeared his face with an insect-repelling sun-block cream before hitting off, wore tinted glasses and a sun-visor, Scanlon was bare-headed and unprotected. His face and nose were pink—a skin-cancer clinician's nightmare.

'This one'll sort you out, son,' Scanlon said. 'You've got the honour.'

The hole was a par three, 167 metres to a large green, bunkered at the front and back. A substantial target, but only to be reached by a shot carrying across at least a hundred metres of water. The land fell away dramatically almost in front of the tee down into a deep chasm where the Pacific Ocean churned and boiled. The rocky ledge on the other side of the gulf, about thirty metres in front of the green, offered no comfort to a short hit—a ball striking it could fly back, left or right, but was unlikely to go towards the pin. Gulls swirled over-head, riding the currents of turbulent air above the water.

'I saw Kel Nagle top his ball into the drink here in a Pro-Am,' Scanlon said. 'Mind you, he put his next shot an inch or two from the hole and still made bogey. Go for your life.'

Dunlop teed up and took out his four iron, put it back and selected a three. The light breeze was blowing to the left to judge from the flag but it could be doing almost anything in the air over the water. The mistake, he knew, was to worry about loft. The green was lower than the tee—the secret would be penetration and accuracy. Ordinarily, hitting over water troubled him, but he was deflected from that

52

by Scanlon's attitude. He took two practice swings, addressed his ball, aimed slightly right, and hit it. The shot carried straight and true across the chasm and was then checked by the wind which seemed to have veered slightly to blow back towards the tee. The ball landed on the fringe, checked and rolled onto the green to finish three metres from the cup.

'Fuck me,' Scanlon said. 'Great shot. What did you do about the wind?'

Dunlop grinned. 'Play your shot, Dave.'

Scanlon teed up and took a four iron. His practice swing was jerky and he hit the ball high and short. It caught the ledge and ricocheted into the ocean. Scanlon thumped the ground with his club. 'Shit. It's fucking years since I did that here.'

As he bent to tee another ball a shout came from behind them. Dunlop turned to see Sammy Tadros running towards the tee. He was waving his mobile phone and sprinting, head down.

'Tell that fucker to shut up,' Scanlon growled. 'I'm trying to line up this shot.' He went through his routine more deliberately and smoothly and hit the ball onto the green. He turned triumphantly, waving his club. Dunlop was listening intently to Tadros. 'Did you see that? I could still get a half.'

Dunlop's face was stern as he walked back onto the tee and picked up his clubs. 'Forget it, Dave. More important things to do. Mirabelle's gone missing.'

7

Detective Sergeant Tillotson's place of work was the new police administration building in Darlinghurst. She had been assigned to a senior post in a unit investigating the potential of 'profiling' as an investigative technique. The method, devised in the United States, involved the careful examination of all evidence found at the scene of a crime with a view to building up a picture of the perpetrator. Tillotson had trained as a nurse prior to joining the police force, and she was reckoned to have the qualifications to assess the usefulness of 'profiling'. She suspected that the appointment had been designed to take her off operational police duties, a move she resented, but she found the work interesting and enjoyed having a number of men as her subordinates.

On the day following her meeting with Kippax and Georges she received a phone call and took an afternoon tea break. She walked along Oxford Street to Taylor Square and was picked up outside the court building by a white, chauffeur-driven limousine. The car sped on towards Centennial Park and Tillotson settled back in the deep leather seat.

The glass panel between herself and her companion and the driver was closed.

'Just you and me, Thomas?' she said. 'But there'd hardly be room for Edgar, would there? Even in a flash car like this.'

Kippax nodded. He wore dark glasses even though the limousine's windows were tinted. 'Edgar has his uses. Impossible to deny that, but he is a shrinking asset, if you'll pardon the expression, Trish.'

Tillotson smiled. 'I know you don't think much of my sense of humour, Thomas. It's not my strongest point, I'm aware, but you don't need to tell me when you've made a joke.'

'Of course not. A small vanity. I don't make many and I was merely drawing attention to it. No matter. Something important has come up which I hope you can handle. How much free time do your present duties allow you?'

'Too much. Office hours, more or less. And flexible at that. I'm used to more activity. I go to a gym, but it's not quite the same.'

Kippax had only the vaguest idea of what going to the gym might mean, and he had absolutely no desire to learn more. 'I imagine not. To business. Scanlon's daughter is missing.'

'Missing from where?'

'From a safe house in Sans Souci.' Kippax glanced at his wristwatch. 'Since early this afternoon. Say, two hours or so.'

'How d'you know this?'

The limousine was cruising along Martin Road with the park on the left. Kippax gazed out at the deep gardens and ornate houses. 'The Witness

Protection Unit is not quite as secure as you seem to imagine. I have a source. The information is good, believe me.'

'As information, it's pretty thin. What d'you want me to do about it?'

'Find her and keep her somewhere safe.'

'Abduct her?'

'Hardly. She's missing, possibly confused and upset. You're an officer of the law. Surely it wouldn't be a problem to keep her incommunicado for a short time.'

'How short?'

'I should think twenty-four hours at the most.'

'I get it. Long enough for you to put some pressure on Dave Scanlon. You must be really concerned about what he has to say, Thomas.'

Kippax stopped looking out the window and turned his head slightly to fix his gaze on Tillotson. 'Trish,' he said and swallowed, 'that is no concern of yours. Scanlon is only one of the items on my agenda, I can assure you. Don't waste your time trying to assess its priority.'

You're lying, Tillotson thought, but she nodded compliantly. 'I can look at Dave's file and pick up some of the stuff I'd need, but there'd have to be a photograph of the girl, a description of her clothes and so on. I take it there won't be a public bulletin put out on her?'

'Not immediately, at least. I'll arrange to get those details to you.' Kippax leaned forward and knocked on the glass partition. The driver's head bobbed and he increased speed slightly. 'This is urgent. Don't draw any conclusions. I may have to go away for a few days. I have a man you can liaise with.'

56

The car turned back in the direction of the city and Kippax resumed staring at the houses, cars and people as if critical of all this activity over which he had no control.

'And who's that?'

'His name is Phillip Krabbe.'

'Any relation to Keith?'

'His son.'

'And he works for you?'

'Not exactly. He'll be in touch with you, Trish. Ah, I think we can drop you here. It looks like rain but you should get back before it starts.'

In fact the first drops fell as Tillotson stepped out of the car. She thought she caught Kippax looking at her legs, but she wasn't sure. She knew he was unmarried and had always thought of him as sexless. Maybe not. She closed the door firmly and watched the limousine pull away. Automatically, she committed the number plate to memory. *I know what you're doing, Thomas,* she thought. *You're putting some distance between yourself and this Scanlon thing. It must be a big deal.* She walked quickly along Oxford Street, contending with other pedestrians for the shelter of the shop awnings. She was often amazed at how transparent supposedly clever men were. *Hard to understand,* she reflected, *how he's riding in a limo while I'm walking in the bloody rain.*

Phillip Arnold Krabbe was thirty years of age, tall and blond, a little fleshy. He had been told that he looked like William Hurt, the actor, and meant to see one of Hurt's movies but had never got around to doing so. He wasn't very interested in movies. His father, paying for his education at Newington College and the University of New South Wales, had automatically assumed that Phillip would join the police force. He had never seriously discussed this with his son, and was astonished when the young man, after his graduation with an LLB degree, announced his intention of going to Harvard to study for an MBA.

'What the fuck is it?' Keith Krabbe had asked.

'A Master of Business Administration.'

'I'm not paying for that crap.'

'I've got a scholarship.'

'How'll you live? Bloody expensive place, New York.'

Phillip did not bother to enlighten his father as to the location of the university. 'I've got some money saved and I'll teach rugby. I've lined up a job at a country club.'

'They don't play bloody rugby in America.'

'They do at this place. Apparently it's very fashionable in New England and the money is good. Also, I'll get the use of the club facilities, which cost the members a bundle. It's a good deal.'

Krabbe grunted. He was becoming confused. New England meant to him the north of New South Wales, and the idea of Americans playing rugby appealed to him as little as Pakistanis playing cricket. Despite his misgivings, he was impressed by his son's plan of action.

'So, when're you going to join the force?'

Phillip had observed his father's career from an early age and overheard many a muted barbecue conference, swimming-pool consultation and late-night telephone call. He was aware that Keith Krabbe was an employee of the state and a functionary for powerful private interests. It was only the latter group that interested him. 'I'm not, Dad. I'm sorry, but I don't want to be a policeman. I want to go into business.'

'Shit. What kind of business?'

'Consulting. Problem-solving.'

'Wanking.'

Relations between father and son improved somewhat when Phillip returned from America with his degree, some money he had acquired by playing the US sharemarket, and abundant self-confidence. Keith Krabbe's stocks, in the meantime, had fallen. The influence of the Roman Catholic clique within the force to which Krabbe had belonged had declined, and it had not taken long for Phillip to see that his father had been sidelined and abandoned by the masters he had served. He set up Krabbe Consulting Pty Ltd and used his father's attenuated name and reputation to make connections with Sydney's business sector. His American gloss, energy and enthusiasm commanded respect. Essentially, he hired talent to deal with problems legal, financial and personal, and charged hefty fees for the results he achieved. He provided a cut-out point between the operatives and the client. His discretion was absolute and his own profile was extremely low.

Getting a commission from Thomas Kippax was his greatest coup to date, and Phillip had decided to deal with it 'hands on'. The element of illegality likely to be involved did not worry him. His heroes were the likes of John Wren, Joseph Kennedy and, until things had come unstuck for him, Robert 'Captain

Bob' Maxwell. Like many of the left-wingers he had known at university, Phillip believed that it was impossible to make a fortune honestly. He was prompted, however, to very different courses of action by this belief from those taken by his socialist acquaintances.

He had set himself a goal—by the age of thirty-three, he intended to have amassed ten million dollars and to have it deposited in offshore accounts safe from tax and auditors. The scheme had seemed feasible in the heady, entrepreneurial eighties, but had proved difficult of realisation. After almost three years of operation, although prosperous, he was a long way from his objective. The right association with Kippax could put him over the line in a couple of moves—and inside his time frame. He wasn't going to hang back out of scruples or fear of complications.

Now, he swivelled on his chair in the Brougham Street office, and looked out over Woolloomooloo Bay. A rainstorm had swept in from the east and darkened the sky, but it was passing and the late afternoon sun was turning the flat surface of the water a silvery green. Phillip was surrounded by the symbols of success—the computerised, carpeted office, the view, the swimming pool shared by the complex of business suites, the courtyard behind the security gate—but he was still the Mick, the copper's son, the reliable half-back, the conscientious but not brilliant student. And he was still hungry.

He switched on his computer and reviewed the data he had been given by Kippax—full description, shoe size and medical records for the missing girl, several photographs (headshots—front and profile, medium and full-length), dental chart, school record, lists of names of friends, hobbies, banking information, credit card purchases over the past six months, library and video borrowings. He had an audio cassette recording of Mirabelle's voice and a short videotape of her walking in the street outside her Randwick home. The availability of this mass of material was unsurprising to Phillip. He would have been disappointed if Kippax had come up with anything less.

He made a telephone call to Detective Sergeant Tillotson and arranged an appointment for her in one hour's time. At the time when most business executives of his standing were looking forward to their first evening drink, Phillip Krabbe changed into swimming trunks and did thirty laps of the short pool. He showered, slicked back his hair and put on a fresh shirt. His beard was light, and when he returned to the office he looked as fresh as if he had just walked in at his customary starting time of eight a.m. He greeted several of his departing employees amiably but with no particular warmth. He found friendship difficult and, so far, love impossible. His Catholic upbringing and his Protestant education, his mother's piety and his father's lubricity had left him confused and inhibited. A non-smoker and light drinker, he kept himself in good physical condition and planned to undertake extensive sexual education after he had made his pile.

Trish Tillotson gave her name to the security guard and entered the courtyard. A discreetly illuminated signpost pointed the way to Krabbe Consulting and she followed it, taking in the plush surroundings, the evidence of money having been spent. Hence, parking space, good security, high rents. She was impressed. As a country girl who had grown up with collapsed fences, rickety star stakes, cars lacking starter motors, she was admiring of city solidity and permanence. She owned a flat in Bellevue Hill, lived modestly and only indulged herself when on holiday because she could not risk demonstrating her growing affluence. This irked her and she liked to see signs of people being able to show what they could afford. It was something to look forward to.

The door to the Krabbe Consulting suite stood open and she walked in, glancing at the desks in the open plan office with their computer terminals, modular filing cabinets and pot-plants. A tall man appeared at a doorway and stood expectantly. He looked young. Interested, she held herself straight and quickened her step. Trish Tillotson had no time for old men. When holidaying in Queensland or the Pacific Islands, she selected young, virile companions and rewarded them well. *Young and successful,* she thought. *That's a change.*

'Detective Tillotson.'

'Mr Krabbe. This's ridiculous,' Trish Tillotson said. 'Trish.'

'Phillip.'

They shook hands. Phillip felt an odd sensation as their fingers met. He wanted to pull his hand back and only just managed to stop himself from doing so. Something about her dry, hard touch disturbed him. It made him feel strangely young and... unmanned. The reason for this came to him in a rush of understanding. Trish Tillotson reminded him of his mother—the same dark, angular features, so unlike his own, and the same burning intensity in her eyes. But this was a woman not significantly older than himself and wearing make-up, a tight skirt, a silk blouse and high-heeled shoes. He was not unmanned, rather the reverse. He felt a throbbing in his groin.

'Is there anything wrong, Phillip?'

'No, no, nothing. Please come in. We have a good deal to talk about.'

She walked past him into his office, smelling shampoo and soap, a touch of chlorine, perhaps. As she entered the office she saw the light reflected off the surface of the swimming pool and she understood the chlorine tang. *Jesus*, she thought, *a working body, not like the slobs I'm usually fending off.* She was picking up vibes with every movement she made. She sat in a chair, let her skirt ride up and let him see her legs if he was interested. He was.

Phillip's throat dried as he sat behind his desk and looked at the woman. Her mouth was a narrow, dark red slash in an olive-skinned face. The sharpness was arresting, exotic. With that colouring you expected thick, heavy features. Phillip was astonished to find himself making these judgements. His practice, on meeting a person of either sex with whom he was to do business, was to assess first brains, then energy, then resourcefulness. What was he doing looking at legs, a mouth, hooded dark eyes, and wondering about the shape of the small breasts under the shimmering blouse and the severe jacket?

Trish Tillotson let her purse drop to the floor and crossed her legs. She could read the signs. This boy-wonder with the million-dollar office was hot for her. Thomas Kippax might have taken a sly look at her legs but Phillip Krabbe was ready to lick them. She felt herself become excited. Male excitement in whatever form it took aroused her. She wrenched her mind away from the possibilities and put her hands on the desk, letting him see her ringless fingers. 'Thomas Kippax,' she said, 'seems to think we can work together to locate this girl. I know how to look, you know exactly what we're looking for. Right?'

Phillip nodded and switched on his computer. 'It's all here.'

'That's good. Before we start, do you know why Thomas wants her found?'

'No, and I have no intention of asking him.'

'What if I was to tell you?'

'Why would you do that?'

Tillotson saw that she had a version of an innocent on her hands. She was slightly disappointed but still stimulated. Innocence needed to be eroded rather than assaulted. 'Good question,' she said. 'Let's see what you've got there, Phillip.'

8

'If you think I'm going to just sit at home while my kid's missing you're crazy,' Scanlon said. 'I'm going to help find her.'

'You'll do as you're bloody-well told,' Dunlop replied. 'This might have nothing to do with your business. If it does, it could be a ruse to flush you out. If it's something else, you'll hear soon enough.'

'You cold-hearted cunt. This's my daughter we're talking about.'

The two men were standing in the driveway of Scanlon's house after rushing from the golf course. It had taken physical action from Dunlop to prevent Scanlon leaping into a car and taking off on his own, and the argument had been going on ever since.

Scanlon's concern was totally genuine, showing in the anxiety with which he chain-smoked and plucked at the blemishes on his skin. Dunlop could not simply drive away and leave him in his agony. 'We don't know enough yet, Dave. Maybe you can help when we've got all the facts. Tell you what I can do, I'll send your wife over and ...'

Scanlon shook his head, dropped his cigarette butt and ground it out under the heel of his golf shoe. The spikes gouged the gravel. 'No, no point in that. Me and Lucy haven't got much to say to each other these days. A thing like this, she'd just blame me and I'd blame her.'

'Maybe that's what the kid was running away from.'

Scanlon lit another cigarette. He had gone without for almost twenty-four hours, but had begged a packet from one of the minders after getting the news about Mirabelle. 'That's a great help,' he said bitterly. 'You blaming both of us.'

'I'm sorry,' Dunlop said. 'I know it's lousy for you. But use your head, Dave. You must've worked on missing kid cases. Did you ever see one where a parent was any use?'

Scanlon straightened his shoulders which had sagged noticeably, reducing his height. He no longer stood his full four inches taller than Dunlop. 'I'll give you a couple of hours. Then I'm going to get to work on it myself and Christ help anyone who tries to stop me.'

It was the old bravado, Dunlop recognised. All the favours due to him had been called in long ago. But in a way, Dunlop was relieved to see fantasy taking over. He had constrained Scanlon easily when he had made his rush for the car and was surprised at the big man's lack of strength. Something had eaten David Scanlon away physically and emotionally, and Dunlop had begun to form a clearer picture of what it was. He lifted the expensive clubs and buggy from the boot of the car and waited for Scanlon to take them. The minders were moving into place around and inside the house.

He attempted a soothing, collaborative tone.

'Soon as I know anything, you'll hear, Dave. And vice-versa. Right?'

Scanlon steadied the golf bag for a moment, then let it fall clattering to the ground. He kicked the buggy so that it careered away into a flowerbed. 'Fuck it,' he said. 'Fuck everything. Fuck you, Carter.'

Dunlop drove to Sans Souci on the speed limit with his golf clubs rattling in the boot. The sound reproached him. Should he have imposed greater security at the safe house? Had it been frivolous to go golfing with the client? Had his pleasure in making contact with Maddy again distorted his judgement? Dunlop was not a reflective man and was not given to self-criticism. He shrugged the questions away and concentrated on what to do next. Obvious. Find the girl. Protect the client. Minimise the damage.

Maddy was waiting for him outside the house. He drew a deep breath and resolved not to get into recriminations, aware that the responsibility was mostly his.

'How's Mum taking it?' he asked. He touched Maddy's hand briefly, hoping she would understand what the slight contact meant.

'Coolly, I'd have to say. She says Mirabelle's taken off before. Scorn for our security would be the main thrust of her comments so far.'

Dunlop kept his voice neutral. 'How did she get away?'

'Easily.'

'Come on, Maddy. You know what I mean.'

'Piecing it together, it looks like she went down to

the boat dock fully dressed. Stripped off, put her gear in a garbag and went into the water. She's an excellent swimmer, apparently. We found the garbag with a damp pair of knickers in it over by the point. Nearly a kilometre away. Pretty good swim.'

'And no-one noticed she was gone?'

'Early on, in the morning, before you saw her, she sat in the motor launch for a while and read. The boat can't be started and there's no dinghy. She went down there again with the book later. The water's uninviting. No-one thought about it. It was a mistake, I'm sorry.'

'Not blaming you. I was slack last night. I should have looked the set-up over more closely.'

'Maybe *that's* my fault?'

'Knock it off, Maddy. Did she take anything apart from her clothes?'

'Nothing, except the book—David Eddings, *Pawn of Prophecy*, if you want to know. Oh, and money. Probably a hundred or so. She wasn't kept short, according to her mother.'

She sounded bitter and Dunlop wanted to comfort her but couldn't. 'Does her mother have any ideas about where she might have gone?'

'No. She's barely interested. What about the father?'

'He was too distraught to ask, but I'll get on to that. She didn't say anything, do anything out of the ordinary?'

'Fuck it, Luke. She was here about twenty hours all up. Who's to say what's normal with her? She seemed much the same to me—bolshy.'

'Right. Look, her father said he got a phone call from her this morning. I suppose someone was listening in on that. Is there a tape? She might have said something useful.'

'Do we have to stand here?'

'No, course not. Let's have a look at the boat. There might be something.'

'There isn't. We've been over it, but you can get some idea of ... I've just remembered, she took a towel. She thought it out pretty good.'

'And wore her knickers,' Dunlop said. 'Modest, that's a comfort. What about the phone call?'

They walked around the house and down the bricked path to the boat dock. Maddy wore jeans, sneakers and a T-shirt. Dunlop was suddenly aware of his golf spikes clacking on the path. He felt ridiculous, untied the laces and kicked the shoes off.

'We have a fuck-up,' Maddy said. 'Turns out Lady Muck had a mobile phone in her handbag and nobody spotted it. Mirabelle must've called on that. Lucy says she made a couple of calls as well, but she won't say who to. Got coy when asked. Shit, I just didn't think of it! I'm too fucking working-class to anticipate people having mobile phones.'

'How did you find out?'

'One of the blokes picked it up on a scanner when she made a call. Just the static, she couldn't get through. She handed it over meek as a lamb. Didn't seem troubled. Nothing worries our Lucy except wearing the same clothes two days in a row.'

They were close to the short wooden pier and Dunlop noticed that the cyclone fence ended a couple of metres before the water. Maddy saw where he was looking. 'Sensors installed in there,' she said. 'There's no sneaking out that way.'

Dunlop nodded and stepped onto the boards. The

sock on his right foot snagged on a splinter and he swore. He moved gingerly to the edge of the planks and looked down at the water. It was murky with a slight oil slick and bits of plastic floating on the surface. 'You're right,' he said. 'I wouldn't fancy swimming in that.'

'I'd like to toss the mother in.'

'She's really getting to you, isn't she?'

'She's not my type, that's for sure. But it's more than that. I get the feeling she knows something I don't. It's giving me the shits.'

'Funny. I've got the same feeling about Dave. He's holding something back.'

'Must've been fabulous fun for the kid, hanging out with two adults who hate each other and whose hobby is keeping secrets.'

Dunlop reached the end of the dock and surveyed the short distance from the ladder to the launch. He jumped and landed lightly on the salt-stained deck. The vessel rocked slightly and he steadied himself by gripping the top of the cabin. A folding chair stood between the cabin and the rail, mostly concealed from anyone looking down from the house or yard. 'Where'd she swim to?'

Maddy pointed to a heavily wooded spit of land sticking out into the water a considerable distance away. The river was calm but he could see the swirl of a current. The water was dark where overhanging trees blotted out the sun. All in all not an inviting prospect, and it would have taken some determination to make the swim. The launch rocked again as Maddy jumped. She joined him by the rail. 'As far as we know, she'd never been in this part of the world before, but she picked the right place to swim to.'

She pointed to a muddy bank, not far from the mooring. 'If she'd gone in there she'd have got nowhere. There's some impenetrable privet and crap further up.'

'The kid can handle herself, it seems,' Dunlop said. 'I'm not sure if that's good or bad.'

'Good, surely.'

Dunlop shrugged. 'The longer she's on the loose the more time for the screws to be turned on Dave. I don't suppose she left a note or anything.' He caught Maddy's look of reproach. 'Sorry. I'm clutching at straws. Well, I suppose I'd better go and talk to Lucy. Pity it wasn't her who did the flit. I don't think he would have given two hoots. And you say the feeling's mutual?'

Dunlop hauled on the mooring rope until the launch bumped against the pylons. He gripped the ladder and followed Maddy back up onto the deck.

'I don't think she hates him,' Maddy said. 'She's more like vaguely hostile. No, that's not it—uninterested, indifferent.'

'D'you think she's interested in anyone else?'

'Apart from herself? Now that's a good question.'

Lucy Scanlon lifted one sculptured eyebrow as Dunlop, carrying his golf shoes, and Maddy entered the sitting room. She was elegantly arranged in a chair, reading a magazine and wearing the dress she had worn the day before but somehow managing to make it look fresh and new. Her slender legs were neatly arranged to advantage, her high-heeled shoes complementing her shapely ankles and her short skirt riding up to mid-thigh.

'Well, we're a little late on the scene, aren't we, Mr Dunlop? Have a good innings or set or whatever it's called?'

'Round,' Dunlop said. 'No, not really. Your husband's a very distressed man, Mrs Scanlon.'

'I can imagine.'

Dunlop sat down in a chair opposite Lucy while Maddy moved restlessly across to stand near the window. 'Can you? What I can't imagine is why you're taking this all so calmly. You know that your lives are in danger and...'

'We knew that when a petrol bomb exploded in our beach house,' Lucy said crisply. 'I lost some irreplaceable things in that little incident.'

Dunlop's temper snapped. 'Things!' he shouted. 'Who the hell cares about things? We're talking about people here—your husband and your daughter. Have you no feelings at all?'

'I'll thank you not to shout. I've had fourteen years of a shouting man and that's more than enough.'

Dunlop was about to shout again when he caught the meaning of her words. 'Mirabelle's sixteen, isn't she?'

'Ah, the man has a brain after all.' Lucy turned her head to look at Maddy, who had stopped fidgeting with a curtain and was looking at Dunlop. 'Got it too, have you, dear?'

Maddy lowered herself slowly into a padded armchair. An ashtray containing several filtered butts teetered and she steadied it.

'Mirabelle's,' Lucy said. 'Do you honestly think I'd allow a daughter of mine to take up that disgusting, mindless habit?'

'She's not your daughter,' Dunlop said.

72

'Give the man a prize. Of course she's not, not in looks, not in brains, not in manners. She's David's child by some little scrubber he rubbed up against somewhere. I lost my child, miscarried, and in a weak moment I agreed to our adopting David's by-blow. I have never ceased to regret it.'

'But you brought her up,' Maddy said. 'You must care for her in some way.'

Lucy shrugged. 'Not a jot. Nor she for me. You must have seen that.'

Dunlop struggled to absorb her information and its implications. 'Does she know you're not her mother?'

'She found out a year or so ago.'

'How?' Maddy said.

'David told her after we'd had an argument. If there had ever been any chance of our having an amicable relationship that ended it. Not that there *was* much chance.'

Dunlop leaned forward in his chair, feeling ridiculous in his stockinged feet. 'All that aside, do you have any idea where she might have gone?'

The elegant shrug again. 'Not the slightest. Nor do I care, and I have to tell you this, *Mr* Dunlop and *Ms* Hardy, that I wish to leave this place at once.'

'I can't permit that,' Dunlop said.

Lucy's small, even white teeth glittered as she smiled. 'You can't prevent it. I have some very influential friends.'

9

Trish Tillotson quickly reviewed the information Phillip Krabbe had on Mirabelle Scanlon and her disappearance.

'Sounds like a pretty resourceful kid, doesn't she?' Phillip said.

'You fancy her looks?'

'Come on, she's a child.'

Trish found this remark comforting. It had been some time since she'd had any satisfactory sex, let alone an agreeable affair. The big, clean-smelling young man sitting beside her in front of the computer screen was shaping as an ideal candidate.

'Whoever it is inside the WPU giving Thomas this information must be very close to the action. See this detail—cash in hand, credit cards. I don't suppose you know who it is?'

Phillip shook his head. He found proximity to this woman, almost physical contact, exciting. She had taken off her jacket and shaken out her hair so that it fell over her narrow, straight shoulders. He wanted to move the hair and slide his hands down from the back of her neck inside her blouse. He felt himself blushing at the thought of doing this. *Gross*, he thought. *Totally unprofessional and offensive*. He forced himself to concentrate on the question. 'No. No idea. Does it matter, Trish?'

'It could. When you work for people like Thomas you find that they only tell you as much as *they* think you need to know. It might be enough, it might not. Have you worked for him for long?'

Phillip shook his head. 'This is the first time. How have you found him?'

'Like a snake, ready to shed his skin or bite off his own tail. He's a very dangerous man. Pardon me for asking, but you seem to be doing pretty well here, Phillip. Why would you want to have anything to do with this dirty business?'

'I wasn't aware that it was particularly dirty. All business is dirty to some degree, anyway.'

'Not like this.'

'I want the money.'

Fair enough, Trish thought. *Your eyes are open and you're fair game*. 'Have you got anything to drink around here?'

'Yes, of course. Whatever you like.'

'Gin and tonic then. You?'

Health-conscious Phillip hadn't drunk alcohol on an empty stomach since his university days, when two cans of beer after a football game would put him on his ear. Now he drank socially and for business reasons only, always carefully. But the slanted dark eyes and the sharp nose and the pointed shapes under the silk blouse blew caution away. 'Yes, why not?'

He got up and went into the service room. He found that he was nervous and clumsy, but he managed to prepare the drinks, even to remember to slice a lemon and drop a piece into each glass. He was finding it increasingly difficult to keep his mind on the task. What was he supposed to be doing here? Providing the policewoman with whatever information she required and reporting progress back to Thomas Kippax. He carried the drinks back and adopted a forceful, businesslike manner. 'Cheers. Now, what else are you going to need? I can get someone to watch those friends' houses. I've got contacts in two of the taxi companies. Maybe she was picked up close to Sans Souci. I could get a scanner to work the area near Scanlon's house in Randwick—see if she makes contact. What do you think?'

Trish Tillotson sipped her drink and sucked on an ice cube. She was thinking that she'd like to unbuckle his belt and take a mouthful of him. She could sense his own interest, but was impressed by his attention to the matter at hand. She knew she'd have to play him carefully. 'Good suggestions, but that'd all take time, Phillip, and we don't have much. What this needs is imagination, an intuitive leap. Are you any good at those?'

Phillip shook his head. 'Afraid not. I'm pretty much a data analysis man myself. Sorry.'

'Willing to try?'

She couldn't keep the double entendre edge out of the question and Phillip hadn't failed to notice it. Imagination might not be his strongest point but he was trained to pick up hints. His mouth dried and he cleared his throat, realising that he sounded like a nervous schoolboy. 'Of course.'

Trish felt she was on her mettle. She scrolled through the data, tapping the keys expertly with her long, thin fingers, hoping for inspiration. 'You have to look for a theme,' she said. 'A pattern, a series of things that add up and give you a clue.'

'What do you mean?' Phillip felt the gin working on him, he moved closer and put his hand lightly on her shoulder.

'I found a missing kid once who'd gone without a trace, apparently. But there were hints in his room. Pictures of lions and, you won't believe this, I got onto it because of a rickety chair.' She turned and favoured him with one of her witch smiles—the dark slash of a mouth opened over slightly spaced, slightly protuberant teeth.

'I don't get it.'

'The back of the chair creaked, the struts were loose. He wanted to be a lion-tamer. He must've messed about with that chair for years and in the end he'd run off to join a circus.'

Phillip laughed. 'Seriously?'

'Seriously.'

He bent down so that their heads were close together and watched the screen images dissolve and re-form as she touched the keys. 'Stop,' he said. 'Go back to her interests. Uh huh. Go on to those credit card purchases. Right. Water and boats. That's the theme. She was last seen on a boat. She swims away. She bought deck shoes and a water-proof stopwatch. Boats.'

'Jesus,' Trish said. 'I think you're right. You're brilliant! Where's Dave Scanlon's boat moored? What's it called?'

Phillip was trembling with excitement. He almost elbowed Trish aside to get at the keyboard. 'Ah, let's see. The *Mirabelle*. God, it's obvious. It's moored at Rushcutters Bay.'

'That's where we'll find her,' Trish said. She pushed her chair back and stood. She was only centimetres away from him now, half a head shorter. She looked up to see his expression and found his face coming down to meet hers. She felt his arms going around her body and she gripped him fiercely. She tilted her head up and their mouths met clumsily, sliding away. They adjusted and kissed passionately. Her lips opened and her teeth pressed forward, bruising him. He returned the pressure and their mouths locked together, tongues thrusting until they had to break to draw breath.

'My God,' Trish gasped.

His hands had moved around from her back and were pressing hard against her breasts. He was breathing heavily and moaning as he felt her moving against him, her flat, hard stomach and pelvic bone grinding into him. Her eyes were bright with triumph. She had him now, without a question of a doubt. She became quite still and eased herself back.

Phillip almost lost balance as the contact was broken. 'What's wrong?'

Trish ignored the blood pounding in her head and the dampness between her legs. She gave him a cool, quick kiss. A mere peck, but her lower lip had split and he tasted wet saltiness. Her tongue darted out and licked the blood away. 'Nothing's wrong, Phillip. Nothing at all. But let's go and get the girl first.'

Phillip's Saab took them to Rushcutters Bay and Trish's police card got them past the security guard at the yacht club. The guard told them where the

Mirabelle was moored and gave them a description of the boat that meant little or nothing to them. 'She's a thirty-foot ketch.'

'What does that mean?' Trish asked.

'Two-master. You can't miss her.'

'Is there anyone aboard just now?'

'I can't say. I only came on duty an hour ago. I can phone her from here if you like. Save you the walk.'

'That's quite all right,' Phillip said. 'Don't bother. The sea air will do us good.'

The guard shrugged. *Sea air*, he thought. *This is no sailor.* He watched the pair stroll down the jetty and take the correct set of steps towards the mooring. Then he forgot them as one yacht owner arrived to show some visitors over his vessel and another complained of a poorly tied-up boat threatening to collide with his. The guard loved boats but hated boat-owners. This sort of trouble could go on into the early hours.

Trish and Phillip stepped over ropes and avoided obstacles along the dimly lit jetty. Lights were showing in some of the boats and they could see people moving around on them. A small party was going on aboard one of the bigger vessels and drunken laughter rang out over the sound of slapping waves, creaking timbers and ropes and the hum of the marina's generator. Phillip took Trish's arm to help her down a set of steps. Despite her heels, she moved easily and confidently and didn't need help. But she let him touch her, feeling his need and responding to it. She hoped this little bitch didn't give them any trouble. Park her somewhere safe, call Thomas, take Phillip home and fuck his brains out. It was going to be a good night.

To Phillip's inexpert eye, the *Mirabelle* was just a medium-sized boat, showing signs of wear and tear. There was a light gleaming from somewhere on board and heavy rock music playing.

Trish nodded. 'She's here.'

'How do we handle this? I suppose she's entitled to be here. It's her father's boat and she hasn't committed any crimes that I know of.'

'She's a missing person and I'm a police officer. You're a lawyer, aren't you? Didn't I see LLB in that string of letters after your name on your letterhead?'

'Yes.'

'That's all we need. More than enough. Let's get down there.'

Trish hitched her skirt up slightly, went down the ladder and stepped onto the almost stationary boat. Phillip followed, conscious of her athleticism and not wanting to look clumsy. Nevertheless, he misjudged the step slightly and his shoes landed heavily on the planking.

Trish hissed at him to be quiet.

'Who's there?'

The girl's head appeared halfway up the steps leading to the cabin below deck. She was wearing only a bra and pants. She lurched, clutched the rail and the words came out slurred this time, louder and more alarmed. 'Who's there?'

'She's drunk,' Phillip said.

Trish stepped forward and held up her card. 'Are you Mirabelle Scanlon?'

'What about it? Who the fuck are you?'

'I'm a police officer. I want you to come with me. Your parents're very worried about you.'

'That's a fuckin' lie. That bitch isn't worried about

80

me, or Dad. Only fuckin' worries about her fuckin' figure and her fuckin' self.'

'That's enough,' Trish snapped. 'You're in no condition to discuss anything. Now...'

'You're lying. I know you're lying. You're out to get Dad, you fuckin' bastards.'

She ducked out of sight and Phillip could hear a rattling inside the cabin below his feet. 'What's she doing?'

'I don't know. Mirabelle! Mirabelle! Come back here! I don't want to arrest you, but I will if I have to.'

The girl charged from the cabin, swarming up the steps. She had a long carving knife in each hand and she slashed at Trish, working the blades crisscross, forehand and backhand. She was very drunk and unsteady but the slashes were desperate and powerful. Trish felt a knife rip the sleeve of her jacket and she backed away, all thought of Phillip forgotten, thrown straight back to her days on the beat in the Cross and Redfern.

'You crazy little cunt! Stop that!'

'I'll kill you!'

Trish retreated until Mirabelle was at the top of the steps, still slashing. She judged her moment and darted forward, swinging her shoulder-bag into the girl's contorted face and landing a kick below her right kneecap. Mirabelle yelled as the bag, heavily weighted with a police pistol, caught her on the jaw and her knee gave way. She tumbled down the stairs, swearing, flailing for balance, not finding it, tripping and screaming as she missed the last steps and fell heavily. Trish followed her down quickly, ready to fend off a knife and deliver another blow if she had to. The girl lay in a crumpled heap with half her body across the bulkhead to the galley-cum-sleeping area.

Trish bent over her. 'Mirabelle. Mirabelle! Oh, no. Jesus Christ.'

'What?' Phillip called from the deck. 'What's happened?'

Trish looked at Mirabelle's open eyes, crazily tilted, and didn't speak. She heard him coming down the steps but her mind had gone blank. A good night had turned bad, very bad. She straightened up and moved away from the body as Phillip reached her.

'Knocked herself out, has she? I'm not surprised. She sounded so drunk. Was that a knife she was waving about?'

'Yes,' Trish said. 'Two knives in fact. Stupid little bitch. And now she's gone and stuck one of them right through her leg, see.'

Phillip almost gagged as he saw the steel protruding through the girl's right calf. There was a lot of blood but it was seeping, not pumping. 'Yes, I see. We've got to get her to hospital, but it's not too serious. Why's she lying like that?'

'Because she's broken her fucking neck.'

10

'I'll call you a taxi,' Dunlop said.

'Luke, you can't!' Maddy stepped between Lucy Scanlon and Dunlop like a referee separating two fighters. 'You can't just let her walk away.'

'Why the hell not?' Dunlop said. 'This woman's no use to us nor to anyone else, I suspect. Her husband wouldn't cross the road for her and I can't say I blame him.'

Lucy rose from her chair with deportment-school grace. 'The New South Wales police force,' she said, 'should be awarded some kind of medal for turning out the most boorish men in Australia, and that's saying something.'

'Get out, you bitch,' Dunlop said.

Maddy shook her head and watched Lucy stalk from the room. She was about to speak when she saw Dunlop's expression. Far from having lost control, he seemed grimly calculating. 'Call her a cab,' he said, 'and make sure one of the people here follows it. I want to know where she goes.'

'You don't think it was an act? That she'll go to the girl?'

'She's the greatest actress born if it was. No, I just

want to keep tabs on her. The kid might have gone to her father's place. I'd better check.'

He telephoned the Randwick house and spoke to one of the minders, who said there had been no sign of Mirabelle.

'How's Dave holding up?' Dunlop asked.

'He's not. He's getting pissed. I think he's going to pieces.'

Dunlop retrieved his shoes from the car, showered and changed. Scanlon was due to give evidence the following day and it sounded as if he might not be in a condition to do it. They could probably stay proceedings for a day or so, give them time to locate the girl. But Scanlon was likely to unravel further the longer she was missing. The operation was falling apart and he felt responsible for not maintaining better security at the safe house. He drank coffee and began to go through the missing persons routine, familiar from his police days—phone the taxi companies, phone the school friends, put the word out discreetly to the police in Randwick and adjacent areas, send a policewoman to Mirabelle's grandmother's flat in Coogee.

The initial responses were all negative.

Maddy said, 'What if she wanted to get in touch with her real mother? I wonder if she knows who she is.'

'Jesus,' Dunlop said, 'that's a beauty. That's a complication we don't need.'

'Just a thought.'

'Yeah. Me, I'm all out of them. I'll need some help with that. There's some sort of adoption register, isn't there? And lists of people wanting to make contact with their kids?'

84

'That's right. And lists of those who *don't* want to make contact.'

'What a world.' Dunlop made numerous phone calls without result.

The officer who had followed Lucy Scanlon's taxi reported that she had returned and was back in her room. Dunlop was too tired to be surprised. 'How come? Did she spot you?'

'Don't think so,' the officer said. 'Plenty of traffic to hide in. Off she went, drove around for a while and then she came back. She says she's afraid, but she doesn't say what of. She doesn't look scared.'

'Okay,' Dunlop said. 'Probably doesn't matter anyway. She was probably just going to check into the Wentworth.'

'I wouldn't say so. Headed for the North Shore.'

Dunlop made a note. The phone rang. Mirabelle's grandmother was alone in her flat. Dunlop was on the point of calling his superiors to brief them and admit his frustration when Tadros, who had joined the Randwick minders, rang through.

'Luke? Sammy. I've been talking with Dave, if you'd call it talking. He got pissed and passed out, but he was going on about the girl. What's her name again?'

'Mirabelle.'

'Yeah, that's the funny thing. He said the name over and over but he said "*the* Mirabelle", like a boat or something. Make any sense?'

Dunlop's fatigue evaporated. 'You bet it means something. Thanks, Sammy.'

He rang off and was scrabbling through a wad of papers when Maddy came in with coffee. 'What's up?'

'You've read the file. What's the name of Dave's boat?'

'The *Mirabelle*.'

'Yeah,' Dunlop snatched at a printout sheet. 'Moored at Rushcutters Bay. You'd better come with me, Maddy. This might need a woman's touch.'

The guard at the marina scratched his head when he saw Dunlop's Federal police card. 'The bloody *Mirabelle*, eh? Popular boat tonight, but if you're looking for the kid you're too late.'

'Come again.'

'A policewoman and another bloke came a while ago and fetched her away. Said she was sick. Looked pretty crook and all. They had to carry her.'

Maddy said, 'Who was the policewoman?'

'Well, I can't say. She showed me her ID, but I didn't take the name in. Sorry.'

'Description,' Dunlop snapped. 'Her and the man.'

'Shit, I dunno. Taller than the lady here and thinner. Dark. That's about all. I was busy at the time—lot of things going on.'

Dunlop looked down the deserted jetty. 'Busy? Here?'

'That's right. There was a bloke complaining about his power supply and another one pissed off about something or other, and I'm here on my own so . . .'

'Okay. When was this?'

'They left about five minutes ago. What's up? I thought it was all right, her being from the police.'

Dunlop swore. 'What about the man?'

'Biggish bloke. Fair-haired, pretty fit. Could've

86

been a sailor to look at him, but he wasn't. Talked about the sea air—here, sea air. I ask you.'

Maddy said, 'Did you see their car?'

The guard nodded. 'Just a glimpse. Dark, foreign job. I don't know much about cars—I'm a boats man. Must've been parked around the corner there. Took off pretty smartish. Are you going to tell me what's going on?'

'No,' Dunlop said. 'Stay here and keep your mouth shut. Where's the boat?'

They followed the guard's directions, trotting along the planks. Dunlop bumped his knee on a bollard and swore violently. Maddy got ahead of him and took the steps and ladders with more grace. 'There it is,' she said, pointing.

They could hear music coming from below decks and see a light at the bottom of a set of steps. Maddy went first and slipped as her foot touched the deck. She teetered and would have fallen except that Dunlop had come down behind her. Her foot slipped again as he steadied her.

'Something wet here,' she said. 'Luke...'

Dunlop crouched and touched a fingertip to the boards. 'Blood. Fair bit of it. What're you doing?'

'I've sailed on these things. Should be a deck light switch around here. Yes.'

A thin light washed over the deck, showing the dark spots that led from the steps to the dock ladder. Dunlop peered down into the cabin and saw more blood and something metallic gleaming on the floor of the galley.

'She was here,' Maddy said. 'That's her kind of music. What's that?'

'A knife.' Dunlop went down to the galley and saw

87

the pool of blood and the marks of feet that had stood in it. The carving knife had no blood on it and was lying as if it had been dropped or thrown.

'What the hell can have happened here?' Maddy pushed past Dunlop into the living area. The music was coming from a Sony portable CD player. A half-empty bottle of Southern Comfort with the top off sat between the CD player and a sticky glass being investigated by a cockroach.

Dunlop was looking at the footprints. The man and woman had been here and someone bare-footed, presumably Mirabelle. Someone was wounded, also presumably Mirabelle, but not with that knife. There was no smell, so not by gunshot. Another knife.

Maddy produced the remains of a towel with a torn edge. 'They bandaged her up and carried her away.'

Dunlop grimaced. 'Shut off that bloody music and see if you can find a torch.'

Maddy hit a button on the player and rummaged around in the galley and beside the bunk. She found a rubber-encased torch and switched it on. The strong beam played on the bloody footprints. 'There's not really a lot of blood,' Maddy said. 'Maybe it wasn't too serious.'

'Maybe.' Dunlop took the torch and examined the steps leading to the deck, then the deck itself and the ladder and the dock above the boat. His face was grim when he returned.

'What?' Maddy said.

'You might be right. Just a flesh wound that they fixed up. But there's another possibility. The blood up there looks as if it could have dripped from clothing, and then there's no more. None at all.'

'Tourniquet. A good bandage.'

'Either that or she's dead.'

'There's not nearly enough blood. There's no reason to think that.'

'Right. Except that every damn thing seems to be going wrong. I'm sorry, Maddy, but you're going to have to handle things here and it's going to be a bitch. You'll have to get it treated as a Federal police case to override the...'

'I know the drill. I've done it before. Where are you going to be?'

Dunlop was poking around in the galley. He found a mobile phone and put it on a shelf beside Maddy, who was scribbling in a notebook. Had Mirabelle called her father? Or anyone else? He resisted the impulse to get Maddy to check. She would. He discovered Mirabelle's wallet lying under the sweaty Guns 'n Roses T-shirt. He opened it and saw the cash and credit cards. A packet of Winfield filters and a disposable lighter were on the bunk together with a flip-top box of tampons. Inside the box were three expertly rolled marijuana cigarettes. Dunlop slipped the box into his pocket. 'I'm going over to Dave's place.'

'What are you going to tell him?'

'I'm fucked if I know,' Dunlop said. 'Any suggestions?'

'Only for you, Luke. You'd better get a grip on yourself or you're going to screw this one up completely.'

Dunlop tossed the phone into her lap and went quickly up the steps onto the deck. 'Check on her calls,' he said.

11

'This is dreadful,' Phillip Krabbe said. He was driving erratically, obeying directions from Trish Tillotson. The blanket-wrapped body of Mirabelle Scanlon was lying on the back seat. 'What are we going to do?'

'Think,' Trish said. 'There's a garage at my place that's never used. We can put her in there and think. Just watch your driving, we don't want to be pulled over for crossing double lines.'

Despite himself, Phillip felt a kind of excitement, almost overriding the fear. Nothing in his life or plans had prepared him for this, but he was close to being exhilarated. After all, they hadn't murdered the girl and his companion was a member of the police force. That had to count for something. *And* he was still excited by her, especially now. So much had happened so quickly, as in a dream. Everything felt slightly unreal. 'God, you're cool,' he said.

Trish's hand moved to his thigh and stroked upwards. 'Did you think it'd be easy, working for Thomas? It's not like running an ad campaign, or doing a consultancy for a government department.'

They stopped at a light and she unzipped his fly

and slipped her hand inside. 'Jesus,' he groaned. 'Be careful.'

'Think about something that doesn't excite you.'

'I can't think about anything except you.'

'Even with a dead kid in the back?'

Phillip accelerated away from the light. 'Yes. Yes. Even so.'

'Good,' Trish said, pulling her hand out. 'I had my doubts about you, Phillip, but they're beginning to go away.'

Phillip was suddenly clearly aware of something he'd dimly sensed. 'You've been in this situation before, haven't you? That's why you're so calm about it. It's part of the job.'

Trish Tillotson was no stranger to death and had dealt out the dose herself several times when occasion demanded. Her own background had been one of underprivilege and emotional and physical neglect, and she was unsentimental about the streetwalkers, parlour girls and criminal fringe groupies she had dealt with. She despised drug addicts and took the view that there was a category of sub-humans who had to be kept in check. Dave Scanlon's daughter fell outside the usual parameters, but she wasn't about to grieve over her. Trish had her eyes set on achieving high rank in the force, early retirement on a good pension with many favours owing to her. She had already accumulated a few, and felt secure in her manoeuvrings with such people as Thomas Kippax. She prided herself on an ability to pick winners, and also to ride them home.

'Turn left,' she said. 'Have you any idea how many people are killed accidentally in this state every week?'

'No.'

'Lots. Scores. Life is dangerous. Everyone's dispensable. The idea that life is sacred is a joke. It can be snuffed out by a leaking brake line, or a bee sting. We're here. Go down that driveway and pull up in front of the third garage door. I'll open it and you can run the car in.'

'Why don't you use it?'

'I don't own a car. I can always get a lift.'

'Won't it seem unusual to the other residents here?'

Trish's hand slid back onto Phillip's leg. 'D'you think you're the first man who's put his car in my garage?'

Phillip gulped. 'I suppose not.'

'You bet not, but I'll tell you one thing—you're the most attractive.'

Phillip nosed the Saab down the dark driveway towards the roller door. Trish left the car, pulled a set of keys from her bag and opened the door. She went inside and flicked on a light. The car crept forward and stopped just short of a pile of tea chests. Phillip switched off the headlights. Trish left the door open and came to the driver's window. 'This is where you decide some things,' she said. 'You can back out of here, drive to the nearest police station and tell them everything that's happened, or you can help me hide her and come inside. Choose, and do it quickly. I have to tell you, the offer's only good for a few seconds.'

Phillip reached back and released the lock on the rear door. He climbed from the car and stood close to Trish. The light in the garage was not strong and the lower half of her face was in shadow. She looked dark and mysterious, slant-eyed and exotic in her rumpled black suit and creased blouse. He noticed a brown streak that had striped her face from eye-socket to jawbone like Indian warpaint, where she had brushed back her hair with a bloodied hand. He touched the mark, feeling her smooth, tight skin and hearing the sharply indrawn breath. The tiny voice, deep inside his skull, telling him to pull out of this madness, fell silent.

'Tell me what to do and I'll do it.'

Trish felt a surge of triumph. She was uninter-ested in equality, stimulated by compliance. 'Behind these boxes.'

The tea chests were empty and Phillip eased them away from the wall as Trish shut the garage door. They lifted the body from the car and put it on the cement floor. Phillip rearranged the chests so that the body was completely hidden from view. All he felt about the inert bundle was that it was surpris-ingly heavy.

The flat was expensively, but austerely appointed, with a minimum of furnishings and appliances. Phil-lip, no connoisseur, had a feeling that the two paint-ings hanging in the sitting room were originals and good. Trish made two gin and tonics and brought them out to the balcony, where there was a view back over parkland towards the city.

'We could go up to the roof,' she said. 'You can see the water from there.'

Phillip gulped his drink and leaned back against the brick wall, which still held a little of the day's heat.

'This is fine. It's great.'

'You're not trying. It cost too much to be called

great. You're nervous—is it about me or what we're doing for Thomas?'

'Both.'

'Action is the best cure for indecision. Who said that?'

'I don't know.'

'Perhaps I did. Anyway, it's true, so let's act.' She took Phillip's hand and led him back into the sitting room, where she produced a hand-held tape recorder. She switched it on and presented it to Phillip. 'Say, "Keep your mouth shut and the girl will be all right".'

Phillip paled. 'I can't say that.'

'Try it. Just for fun.'

'Fun?'

'Wrong word. Just pretend you're dictating to your secretary.'

Phillip took the recorder and closed his eyes. Speaking slowly he said, 'Keep your mouth shut and the girl will be all right.'

'Good.' Trish rewound the tape and pressed several buttons on the machine. When she replayed it the voice was deeper with the vowels flatter. She wound the tape back again, lifted the phone and dialled. When the call was answered she played the tape, hit the STOP button and hung up the phone.

'They'll be listening and they'll record it,' Trish said as she erased the tape. 'But that's several electronic interferences with your voice plus telephone transmission. Unrecognisable, unidentifiable. Now, we've attended to Thomas's business for the time being. Come in here.'

She led him into the bedroom, peeled back the cover to reveal black satin sheets with white pillows.

94

Phillip reached for her but she pushed him away. 'We're going to take this slow and easy. A first fuck's a very important thing and it's idiotic to rush it and mess it up. Don't you agree, darling?'

Phillip nodded nervously. Never sexually aggressive, he had endured enough humiliating episodes of impotence, especially in first encounters, to be willing to be guided by someone with more confidence and experience. She slipped off her jacket and gestured for him to do the same. He did. Then she unbuttoned his shirt, pulled it from his trousers and ran her hands over his chest. She plucked at his nipples, leaned close and teased them with her teeth and tongue.

'Do the same to me.'

Somehow, Phillip's clumsy fingers unfastened the blouse and the brassiere. He trembled at the sight of her small brown breasts, firm and up-tilted with large dark nipples. She stroked his hair as he nuzzled at them, groaning as his teeth closed and his tongue teased the erectile tissue. She unbuckled his belt and pulled down his trousers and underpants. Phillip found trouble with the waistband of her skirt and she helped him with it, crooning and rotating her hips slightly to wriggle out of the skirt and panties. She wore a suspender belt supporting dark-tinted stockings. Her thighs were narrow and hard, almost scrawny. Her crotch was shaven so that her sex was a long, gaping pink fold. She closed her legs on Phillip's probing hand.

'What if I said that's enough,' she whispered. 'What would you do?'

Phillip mumbled incoherently. Her hand had closed around his penis, stroking gently.

'Oh, please, no, don't…'

'You want me?'

'Yes. Yes.'

'You want *me*!'

'Yes.'

'What do you want to do?'

'I want … I want …'

'No, you don't. You want to look and touch. That's all.'

'No.'

She eased away from him, kicked off her shoes and lay back on the bed. Phillip bent to remove his shoes and socks. He crawled onto the bed and attempted to manoeuvre himself on top of her.

'Hold your cock,' she said.

'Wh… what?'

'Hold your lovely cock. See what I'm doing.'

She had put two fingers inside herself and was stroking her clitoris, exposing it as it engorged, pressing the lips of her vagina aside.

Phillip's erection stiffened further as he watched her. She pushed him slightly so that he rolled onto his back. She rose above him and took his penis in her hand, guided it towards her.

'You're ready,' she said.

As he entered her she wet two fingers and slid them up into his anus. Phillip shouted and came immediately in two arcing thrusts.

She let her weight sink onto him. 'Move and you're a dead man,' she hissed.

She bore down, grinding, pressing, swivelling until the movement was painful for Phillip and he shouted again. She kept on and rode forward so that one of her breasts pushed at his mouth. He sucked it in and bit hard, inflicting pain and experiencing it. She screamed as he bit her and gripped his testicles. He orgasmed again, bellowing in ecstatic agony, and she came with him, shuddering and moaning. 'Yes, ah yes. Thank you, thank you. Yes. Yes.'

12

Dunlop called the Randwick house as soon as he got on the road. There was no answer and he began to worry and to increase his speed. He was tired and his nerves were stretched from the events of the day and he drove poorly, narrowly avoiding a collision as he took a turn too wide. He tried the number several times again with the same result and was fearing the worst when he cruised past Scanlon's house. It had happened once before—a house containing two witnesses under his protection had been located by the persons being testified against. Dunlop recalled the feeling of entering the house after being called away by what turned out to be a diversionary tactic. The house had a quality of emptiness he would never forget. The witnesses were never seen again.

Interior and exterior lights were on and the security gate stood open. Dunlop parked on the other side of the street and scouted the corner block carefully. All appeared to be quiet but he couldn't understand the open gate. He edged along the high wall and peered around the gate pillar. Scanlon's red Mercedes and the minders' blue Falcon were in garage slots with the motor scooter alongside them. Dunlop tried the number again and heard the phone ringing inside the house, but there was no reply. He replaced the phone with his pistol, bent low and went through the gate. He worked his way up the side of the drive, moving silently on the tanbark using the cover of the shrubs and flowers.

He reached the garage, cursing silently as he misjudged a step and crunched once, loudly, on the gravel. He looked back down the drive and could see signs of another vehicle having been driven in recently. A van, to judge from the tracks. Other marks indicated wheeled equipment having been unloaded—the swimming pool cleaner. His own tyre marks were clearly visible. No others. The bonnets of both cars in the garage were cold. The lights in the house seemed to come from perhaps three rooms. Dunlop tried to remember the layout—the games room, probably, the main sitting room and the kitchen. He left the garage, keeping to the shadows, and inspected the pool area and adjacent lawn and garden. A light breeze stirred the tops of the tall trees growing alongside the high cyclone fence. A few plastic practice golf balls lay on the lawn alongside a bucket, and a club rested against a pool chair. Otherwise, nothing.

Dunlop slipped across to the back door of the house and eased it open. His sense of smell, acute since he stopped smoking, detected liquor, tobacco, fried food. He moved through the kitchen into a hallway, keeping close to the wall with his pistol held ready. There were more lit rooms than he had thought. A beam of light showed under a bedroom door and he listened at it but heard no sound. He crouched and pushed the door open. The door swung with a soft sigh and Dunlop looked into what was obviously Mirabelle's room—three-quarter bed, posters on the walls, TV and VCR, CD player, videos and discs. An indentation on the bed suggested that someone heavy had sat there since it had last been made up.

The games room was at the end of the hallway and the door was closed. Dunlop turned the handle and let the door drift half-open while moving back out of the line of fire in the approved fashion. He heard harsh, staccato breathing.

'Sammy? It's Dunlop.'

No response.

'Fuck it,' Dunlop said. He kicked the door fully open and went in. Sammy Tadros was lying on the floor, ashen-faced and unconscious. The right side of his shirt was blood-soaked from shoulder to waist. The laboured breathing was his. Another minder, George Bracken, sat in a chair beside the pool table. His arms were drawn behind the chair's back and his ankles were taped to its legs. Four strips of wide tape across his face left only his nose and eyes uncovered. No sign of Barton, the third minder.

Dunlop put his pistol on the green baize and strode across to Bracken. He ripped a strip of tape away from the man's mouth. 'Where's Scanlon?' he shouted.

'He's...'

A movement behind him made Dunlop turn, but not in time to prevent Scanlon from getting between him and his pistol. Scanlon held a shortened, double-barrelled shotgun, its stock cut down to pistol-grip size, in his meaty, freckled fist. 'I'm right here, Carter. Dunlop, sorry. And I'll kill you if I have to.'

'Jesus, Dave. What the hell d'you think you're doing?'

'Well, so far, I've put a bullet in your mate here and got this other bloke to do as he's told. What happens next is more or less up to you. Have you found my little girl?'

Dunlop shook his head. The truth.

'No, and you don't give a fuck either, do you? Just so long as you get me up there singing. Well, things've changed a bit.'

'That's not true. We've got people ...'

'Don't shit me. I know what goes on. I've been in it for over twenty fuckin' years, remember?'

'Calm down, Dave. This isn't going to do any good.' Dunlop forced himself to abandon the rigid stance he'd taken when Scanlon appeared. He was calculating his chances of getting to the shotgun. Scanlon had been said to be drunk but there were no signs of drunkenness now. The heavy, badly balanced weapon was held very steadily. He pointed to Tadros. 'How bad is he hit?'

Scanlon shrugged. 'He's got a .22 slug in the shoulder and another one seems to have nicked a lung. He'll be all right. You only need one bloody lung, last I heard.'

Bracken's voice was a thin, broken reed, forced out between lips puffed and abraded by the heavy tape. 'He didn't have to shoot Sammy. He panicked.'

'That's how much you know, son,' Scanlon said coolly. 'He had his chance, but he wasn't fucking good enough.'

Dunlop wanted to encourage talk, giving him the possibility of deflection. He winked at Bracken. 'I thought I told you to search the house for guns.'

101

Scanlon chuckled. 'Finding one gun doesn't mean you've found them all. Did you ever meet a cop who didn't know how to hide a gun... Luke?'

Dunlop became aware that it was Scanlon who was orchestrating the proceedings, not himself. The big man scooped up Dunlop's pistol and checked it over expertly by touch while keeping the shotgun levelled and his eyes riveted on Dunlop's face. Satisfied, he put the shotgun on the pool table and covered Dunlop with the pistol. 'Fuckin' thing was getting heavy.'

'Okay, Dave,' Dunlop said. 'What's the next move? Sammy needs a doctor if you don't want to face a murder charge.'

'I've faced one already. Wasn't too bad. Don't make any mistakes, mate. I'm not expecting to face any charges of any fucking kind. This is all going to end pretty soon, and surviving it's not my top priority.'

'That's crazy,' Dunlop said.

'Everything's crazy. Snatching an innocent sixteen-year-old girl to threaten her lousy, corrupt bastard of a father. You don't think that's crazy?'

'You've been contacted?'

'You bet I have. You think I've done all this just because I got impatient?'

'I can help you, Dave. Put the gun down. Let's talk.'

Scanlon put the muzzle of the pistol to Bracken's temple. Bracken's eyes opened in terror and he jerked his head away. Scanlon dug the metal in hard. 'You want me to prove I'm serious?'

Dunlop's hands went up involuntarily in appeal. 'I know you're serious,' he said.

'Right. Now this is the way it's going to be. I know

who's behind this and why. That's what you wanted to find out, isn't it?'

Dunlop nodded, judging the distance and Scanlon's likely reflexes. Too far, too fast.

'Before I shut him up, George here told me what a great operator you were, and how you like to play by your own rules. The word is you blew Kerry Loew away because you were fucking his missus. Is that right?'

Dunlop relaxed, eased a little closer, said nothing.

'I can understand that. The times I went crazy over some slut or other and fucking near tossed everything away ... Well, it doesn't matter. The point is, we can work together on this and get a hell of a lot further than by me whistling "Danny Boy" to a mob of bloody lawyers.'

Dunlop looked at Tadros, whose colour and breathing were getting worse. He didn't have a choice, but, oddly, he didn't want one. Something about Scanlon's determination and steadiness encouraged him to think that they *could* work together. If Scanlon knew things he didn't know the reverse was also true—the guilty knowledge about the damage done to Mirabelle was eating at him. Like her father he felt he had to *do* something. Going through channels after this day's cock-ups would involve him in waist-deep paperwork. The part of Dunlop's nature that had made him a rogue cop and an improviser as a WPU officer was uppermost.

'Okay, Dave. I'm with you, provided we get help for Sammy first and fast.'

'Christ, I hope I can trust you.'

'You can.' Dunlop was surprised to find that he meant what he said.

103

'I'm sorry about the wog, but he should know the difference between a man who's pissed and one who's pretending. Do what you like with these two, I've got a few things to collect. See you outside in five minutes.'

Scanlon hesitated, then tossed the pistol to Dunlop. He picked up the shotgun and left the room. Dunlop heard Bracken's sigh of relief. 'You can take him, Luke,' he said.

Dunlop untied the rope around Bracken's wrists and ankles. 'I'm not even going to try. What happened to the other bloke?'

'Sammy reckoned Dave was too pissed to worry about. He let Barton go home and see his wife.'

'Shit. All right, George, get on the blower and get help for Sammy.'

Bracken massaged his wrists and limped towards a telephone. 'What're you going to do?'

'I'm going with Dave.'

'Do I tell them that?'

'Yeah, and tell them Mr Scanlon probably won't be testifying tomorrow. Get busy.'

Bracken dialled and Dunlop bent down to examine Tadros. His pulse was strong and the bleeding had stopped. Tadros was built like a bull and would survive. As he straightened up and heard Bracken giving directions, he wondered about Mirabelle Scanlon. This case had fallen badly apart and was claiming casualties; he hoped that the most innocent person involved was not the worst of them.

Scanlon stood by Dunlop's car with an overnight bag at his feet.

'What's in there, besides the shooter?' Dunlop said.

'Not much. Let's go.'

They heard the ambulance siren before they were a block from the house. Scanlon looked back at the winking red lights. 'Good house, that,' he said. 'I'm going to miss it.'

'Burning your bridges, Dave?'

'Something like that. Let's get moving.'

'Where're we going?'

'Just drive. Let's get this settled first.'

Dunlop's mobile phone rang and he ignored it. He drove in the direction of the city and told Scanlon that he had found where Mirabelle had hidden and that she had been taken away by a man and a female declaring herself to be a policewoman. 'You were muttering the name of the boat when you were pissed. You must have sobered up awfully fast.'

'I did.'

'Why was that?'

'Something occurred to me. Was Mirabelle all right when they took her?'

Dunlop sensed that Scanlon would detect a lie. 'We found blood, Dave. Not a lot and we couldn't tell whose. They carried her.'

'Bastards. Descriptions?'

Dunlop shook his head. 'Not good ones. Nothing much on the bloke. Big, fit. The woman was dark and skinny. That's about all.'

Scanlon said nothing and stared through the windscreen for several minutes. He took a packet of cigarettes from his pocket, found it was empty, swore, wound down his window and threw it out. 'I'm going to kill Kippax if anything's happened to Mirabelle. Get that straight. He's a scumbag like his brother. Neither one of them's any loss.'

'I'm not sure you could negotiate immunity for killing both Kippaxes.'

'I'd get immunity. I'll give you another name. Chief Inspector Edgar Georges. Just think of the tales Edgar'd tell with his nuts in the wringer. And don't forget your old mate Ian McCausland. You'd like to see Ian up to his neck in the shit, wouldn't you?'

'You bet I would! Did he actually do the hit?'

Scanlon ignored the question. 'I should have sent her away somewhere, but that would've sent Kippax a message. It's your fucking fault for letting her loose. I should've known this Witness Protection stuff was Mickey Mouse bullshit.'

Dunlop chose his words carefully. 'It should have been tighter, you're right. Things go wrong. Look what happened back at your place. If it means anything to you, Dave, she did a bloody good job of skipping out. You're right there, too. You can't hold on to anyone who wants to get away, not if they're smart.'

Scanlon hawked, cleared his throat and spat from the window. 'Suddenly, I'm smart, am I? Shit, I feel lousy. You want to ring in about your mate?'

Dunlop shook his head as he slowed deliberately to bring the car to a stop at another light. 'He'll be all right. They're not the first bullets Sammy's taken. He told me once his dad was one of those maniacs who caught slugs in his teeth. Carnival act in the old country or somewhere. Got hit a few times in *that* game, I'll bet. So, it's in the family.'

Scanlon laughed harshly.

Dunlop drove quietly away from the lights and glanced across at his passenger. The weatherbeaten face looked drawn. His left eyelid twitched and sagged. 'I talked to a doctor about you, Dave.'

Scanlon was chewing at his lower lip. 'Yeah?'

'He reckoned you were a heart attack or stroke case, waiting to happen.'

'Fuck him. I'll last long enough to get Mirabelle safe, and that's about all that matters in my shitty life.'

Dunlop was driving along Cleveland Street, heading towards Victoria Park. He took a left turn and pulled up in a small side street.

'What the fuck are you doing?' Scanlon growled.

'I'm sick of driving nowhere.'

'I've been trying to think.'

'So, give me the results.'

Scanlon sighed, unzipped his bag and took out a tape recorder. He pressed a button and a voice filled the car: *Keep your mouth shut and the girl will be all right.*

'Electronically modified,' Dunlop said, 'over the phone and recorded again our end. His voice probably sounds entirely different. Sophisticated stuff.'

'Kippax has the best, so does the police department. We've got two ways to go and I can't make up my mind.'

Dunlop rubbed his hand over his face and felt the rasp of his whiskers. 'Look, I'm tired. I've been outsmarted a couple of times today and I've got no pride left. If you've got two ways to go, for Christ's sake tell me about them, because I haven't got a bloody clue.'

'The policewoman at the yacht club could've been Trish Tillotson. It figures—Kippax, Loomis, Tillotson. The description fits her.'

'It's hardly a description. Still, okay. What's the second thought?'

'How did they know Mirabelle was on the loose? Who told them? Who was running the safe house? You must have a leak. That's what hit me back when I was getting pissed. I thought you and me could put on a bit of pressure.'

Dunlop ran the names, faces and records of Maddy's colleagues rapidly though his mind. He felt confident of all of them. Then the realisation hit him—Lucy Scanlon had had a mobile phone and the opportunity to make calls *after* Mirabelle had taken off.

13

Trish Tillotson and Phillip Krabbe made love three times in the space of little more than an hour. They were both exhausted after the third occasion and fell sweatily asleep, wrapped together in the tangle of satin sheets and covers that had come adrift from the mattress and pillows. Phillip awoke first, startled to find himself in a strange bed with a red-tinted light shining into his eyes. At some point in the proceedings, Trish had turned on the light which gave her naked body a metallic glow. She had got Phillip to remove her stockings and had tied his wrists to the bedposts with them. She had lowered herself onto him, teasing by lifting herself almost clear then easing down again. The third time he had entered her from behind. He looked at her as she slept. There were fine lines around her eyes and mouth, visible now that the light make-up she wore had been eroded.

She woke up suddenly as his hand wandered towards her crotch.

'What are you doing?'

'I just wanted to touch.'

'Touch then.'

He stroked her and she moaned, thrusting herself at his hand. He lifted himself up but she shoved him, collapsing his elbow, forcing him down. 'Don't be selfish,' she said. 'Do it to me.'

She was still slick with his semen. He rubbed and probed, falling into a rhythm with her writhing and thrusting. She whimpered softly as she came and then lay back with her dark, damp hair fanned out on the white pillow. 'That's one I owe you.'

Phillip had not given the events of the night a thought since entering the bedroom, but they came into his mind, sharply and full of threat, as his erotic arousal waned and he emerged from what felt like a sex-induced trance. Trish held his hand clamped to her crotch and she appeared to be drifting back to sleep. Phillip was wide awake, fighting terror. He faced prosecution, possibly gaol, disbarment and disgrace, and for what? He was unsure of the answer. Was it for the wealth he could win from his association with Thomas Kippax, or the amazing favours to be had from the woman lying next to him? Surely both, and which was the more important hardly mattered.

'What's on your mind, lover?' Trish's voice was husky and rough, her usually carefully enunciated vowels had slipped.

Phillip lied. 'Mind's a blank.'

'Bullshit it is. You're worried about little Miss Yacht Club down there in the garage. No, not her really—you're worried about your wonderful career and your bright, shining future. What was it going to be, Phillip—your future?'

'A great deal of money, very quickly, and then... I'm not sure now.'

'Doesn't sound like much of a plan, but I like the sound of the money. You can still make it, don't worry. It all comes down to how we play Thomas Kippax. Why d'you think he was willing to go this far... well, a long way anyhow, to get hold of the girl?'

'Her father must have something very telling. Evidence of some kind.'

A light breeze crept in under the blind and stirred the sex-laden air in the room. Trish shivered. 'Sydney's too cold for me. I'd like to be somewhere hot, really hot. Spain. Have you ever been there?'

'Yes.'

'Is it hot?'

'Some of the time.'

'Not good enough. Might be better to travel. Go to all the hot places so you never had to wear clothes, or only little bits. How does that sound?'

Phillip looked at her whiplike body, coppery under the coloured light. Gymnasium-conditioning had shaped her flat stomach. He remembered the pinioning strength of her sinewy thighs and the grip of her long-muscled arms. Incredibly, he wanted her again. He would do a lot to keep her. 'It sounds wonderful, but what do you mean by *playing* Kippax?'

'I want to know what David Scanlon knows. Otherwise, Thomas holds all the cards.'

'You mean blackmail him? That's a very serious offence, very dangerous.'

Trish laughed and lifted herself up on one elbow. One small, brown-tipped breast jutted towards Phillip. He wanted to touch it but her expression was concentrated and fierce. 'You think so? How many prosecutions for blackmail can you recall in this state in recent years?'

'I see,' Phillip said.

'Doesn't mean it doesn't happen. It happens all the time. In politics, say. That's just one great big blackmail from start to finish. Police work's the same. How many crimes d'you think would get solved without informers?—and they're *all* being blackmailed, one way or another. Your father was a past master at all this stuff.'

Phillip smiled. 'Was he?'

'What's funny?'

'Nothing. It's just that I've spent most of my life trying to be unlike my dad. Studying, going abroad, not going into the police force. And here I am playing the same game, according to you. I guess you can't escape your breeding, or upbringing.'

Trish shrugged. 'It's the sharp end. The real world. The way things happen. Most people have absolutely no idea of what goes on. Some of the investigative journalists get a sniff of it from time to time, but the game's set up so that they can't publish what they find out. Anybody who thinks in terms of the fair go is a bloody idiot. Expect the worst and do your best for yourself—that's my motto.'

'And if the worst happens?'

'Don't whinge about it.'

Keith Krabbe had never been given to philosophising, but Phillip suspected that what Trish had stated approximated his father's position. He found it persuasive—play for the high stakes and accept the risks. His previous strategy suddenly seemed overcautious and dull and he realised that he'd been moving in this direction as soon as he'd accepted the

112

commission from Thomas Kippax. There was a frisson in the thought that Kippax himself was now only just another player, not the maker of the rules. He felt a need to prove himself; he wouldn't hold this woman's interest just because the sight, smell and touch of her made blood flow to his cock.

'So we have to get hold of Scanlon somehow, *before* Thomas knows about it.'

And eliminate him, most probably, Trish thought, but she didn't say so. She kissed Phillip hard with her bruised, split mouth, enjoying the pain. 'That's right. We have to get Dave to come to us, and from what I know of him, he's not going to sit quietly in some safe house after getting that message. He'll come looking.'

'For Kippax?'

Trish frowned; deep furrows appeared in the tight skin between her eyes and the effect was disturbing, as if the workings of her brain were being exposed. 'That's logical to expect, but I'd like to deflect him in my direction. It's about time I contacted Thomas, anyway. Would you make some coffee, and put a shot of brandy in it? You'll find everything you need in the kitchen.'

'You don't want me to hear the call.'

A sensual, puffy-lipped smile replaced the frown. 'I'm protecting you, darling. Trust me.'

Thomas Kippax slept poorly at the best of times, and worse when under stress. He was in no more than a light, troubled doze when the bedside telephone rang. He reached for it eagerly; sleep was unproductive. 'Kippax.'

'I don't think I have to identify myself, do I?'

'As you wish.'

'We, the liaison officer and myself, have the merchandise and contact has been made with the buyer.'

'Good, but I can assure you that this is a secure line. There's no need...'

'Very well. When Dave Scanlon hears what's happened he'll want to come after you in some way. I want him to be deflected to me in the first instance.'

'Isn't he... under protection?'

'That won't stop Dave. Now, I'm guessing he'll make contact with Edgar Georges. What you should do is talk to Edgar and get him to steer Dave towards me.'

'Why?'

'I can handle Dave. I can really put the screws into him. Will you do as I say?'

Kippax reflected. The woman was putting herself directly into the firing line—for a reason, presumably. He could see no present danger in it. 'Very well. The merchandise is safe?'

'Oh, yes. Very safe. I think you're going to be very happy with the results.'

'I trust so.' Kippax plumped up a pillow; he was beginning to enjoy himself. 'Do you think the SCCA schedule as presently set will stay in force?'

A pause.

'I think not.'

She knows a hell of a lot more than she's letting on, Kippax thought. *But then, so do I.* 'Good. Was there anything else?'

'No. Good night.'

Kippax hung up and then dialled Edgar Georges'

number. He took a malicious pleasure at the thought of the fat policeman being awakened from a no doubt deep and drunken sleep.

'So,' Scanlon said. 'Any ideas?'

Dunlop had to think fast, difficult in his tired, confused state. He decided that he needed every edge on Scanlon he could get, and the suspicion about Lucy was a definite edge. He shook his head wearily. 'No. I'd swear they're all okay. Maybe someone spotted Mirabelle in Rushcutters Bay. Who knows?'

Scanlon hammered the dashboard with his fist. 'Fuck it. I thought there might be a fast way. Okay, if we have to get to Kippax through channels we'd better go and see Edgar Georges. D'you know Edgar?'

'I know the fat bastard,' Dunlop said slowly, 'and I don't like him.'

'Me either. That could almost make it fun if it wasn't for Mirabelle. Edgar's got a fancy place in Paddington. I think I can find it. We're going to have to stop for some smokes though.'

Dunlop started the engine. 'Why not go straight for Tillotson?'

'Because I don't know where the bitch lives. Not many people do. But fat Edgar's one who does.'

14

Edgar Georges' immense belly pressed hard against the elasticised waistband, stretched to the limit, of his black silk pyjamas. He'd been asleep when Kippax rang and the conversation had been so brief and so quietly conducted that his wife had not stirred. Georges had got up, urinated, and mixed himself a brandy and soda. He was going to need something to sustain him through a visit from a badly stirred-up David Scanlon. He stood at the downstairs bay window in what he called the den of his terrace house, holding his drink in one hand and meditatively scratching his crotch with the other. The street was leafy and quiet. Two of the things he'd paid a bundle for back when the real estate market was booming. It sometimes irked him to think that he'd never get what he'd shelled out for the house, not this century. Georges didn't like being taken for a mug. Not that he intended to sell. He'd retire to the place at Horse Bay in a couple of years and keep this as his city base. He tried to remember the French phrase the agent had used. Couldn't. Sipped on his drink. A .38 automatic was under a cushion in his favourite armchair—

the one upholstered in beige leather with the smoker's stand beside it.

He crossed the room, opened a drawer in a roll-top desk and spread some papers on the desk top. Then he ripped the cellophane from a packet of Rothman's filters, took out a cigarette and put it in his mouth. He placed the packet on the pale leather covering the arm of the chair and returned to the window. A few minutes later, he saw the Laser drive past, heard it stop and turn at the end of the street and watched it park almost directly opposite. The passenger got out—Scanlon, looking eager but edgy, carrying a bag. The driver's head was down, swivelling, cautious.

Fucking lucky to find a spot, Georges thought. *But then, Dave Scanlon always was pretty lucky, up till now.* Georges lit the cigarette, took a drag and put it in the ashtray on the stand. He balanced his glass on the beige leather and went to the door. There was the sound of the gate opening and footsteps on the path, coming up to the porch, crossing the tiles. He opened the door before a knock or a ring sounded. The twin dark holes at the end of a sawn-off shotgun stared back at him.

'Jesus, Dave.'

'Shut up, Edgar, and back up, or your guts'll be dripping down the wall.'

Georges backed into the den. Kippax had told him to resist, appear reluctant, even alarmed. The advice wasn't necessary. Scanlon was dishevelled, unshaven, wild-eyed. He held the brutal-looking weapon rock-steady. Georges flopped down into his chair and picked up his cigarette. His pistol was only inches away but it might as well have been a mile. He recognised the other man now—Carter, going by some other name. Trish Tillotson had known it. In the witness protection game now. *What the fuck was he doing, letting Dave Scanlon run around with a shooter like that?* Suddenly, Edgar Georges was very afraid. He drew on the cigarette and reached for his glass. Scanlon was looking suspiciously around the room, taking in the expensive furniture, the bar, the gilt light fittings.

Scanlon moved towards the bar. 'Having trouble sleeping, Edgar?'

'That's right. I...'

Scanlon's arm flung wide. Held one-handed, the shotgun smashed several bottles and decanters on a shelf behind the bar. Glass flew and the smell of spilt liquor saturated the air.

Georges glanced at the other man. *Dunlop, that was it. Surely he wouldn't let this go on.* But Dunlop hadn't moved. Georges' hand was shaking as he raised the glass to his mouth. He sipped and the drink tasted flat. His throat was dry with fear and he drank some more. 'What's this about, Dave?'

Scanlon laughed harshly. 'You want a drink, Luke? Edgar's having one. Could be his last.'

'No,' Dunlop said. 'Get on with it.'

Georges' mind raced. *These two hard cases are in something together. Get on with what? An execution?* Involuntarily, his weak bladder emptied, soaking his pyjama pants and sending a thin trickle of urine across the leather seat so that he was sitting in a pool of piss. *Don't let me die like this. Don't let me die at all.*

'Dave, please...'

The shotgun came up, levelled itself at his quivering, cascading chins as he drew away from it.

'My daughter,' Scanlon said. 'Someone's taken her.'

It took every ounce of Georges' scant remaining courage not to babble. 'I... heard something about it.'

'You would,' Scanlon said, 'since Thomas Kippax hears about everything and you only shit when he tells you to. Unless you're scared. Scared now, Edgar?'

'Stop it, Dave,' Dunlop said. 'This isn't helping. Ask him or do him, one or the other.'

'I reckon he knows where she is,' Scanlon said.

'No, no... All I know is...' The cigarette dropped from Georges' fingers and rested on the chair arm where it burnt a hole in the leather. Dunlop picked it up and squashed it out in the ashtray.

'Ever see what one of these does up close, Edgar?' Scanlon said. 'Of course you have. Long and distinguished career like yours. It's DOA, isn't it? No worries. Now, let's hear it.'

Georges drained his glass. He was suddenly terrified that the information he had to impart might not be enough. He hadn't expected it to be as bad as this. *I'm too old for this shit.* He tried to make eye contact with Dunlop, to plead with him silently, but Dunlop had turned away to wipe his hands on the bar towel and look at the wreckage.

'Trish Tillotson,' Georges blurted.

Scanlon's left hand caressed the underside of the shortened barrels. 'Go on.'

'She went looking for the girl. That's all I know, I swear.'

Sweat was pouring from Georges' face, seeping into the collar of the pyjamas. He had delivered the

119

message as instructed by Kippax and Scanlon appeared unsatisfied. There was only one thing to add and he couldn't volunteer it, had to wait to be asked.

'I hear that Trish's got a sidekick—big, fit-looking bloke. I always thought she was a dyke, didn't you?'

Georges' mouth was too dry to enable him to speak. He nodded, then shook his head. He had no answer to that one. *Ask me, fuck you! Ask me!*

'Any idea who that bloke might be, Edgar?'

Georges managed a croak. 'No.'

'All right. Now, where do I find Trish?'

Georges struggled to prevent the relief from showing on his face. It wasn't too hard to do, sitting with his balls in piss and his glass empty and the hole in his precious chair. The ludicrous thought that he'd need a new leather chair came to him just before he spoke. 'The trainees' hostel. She's a …'

The shotgun jabbed forward. 'Don't play games with me, Edgar. Where does she fuckin' *live*?'

'Bellevue Hill. Flat 4, 26 Hickson Street.'

'Phone?' Dunlop said.

Georges shook his head. 'Dunno. Dave, I …'

'Shut up,' Dunlop snapped. 'What's that?'

'Edgar?' The voice came from above them.

'My wife,' Georges said.

Scanlon was putting the shotgun back in the zippered bag. 'I feel sorry for her,' he said. 'Keep her quiet.'

Georges rose from the chair and waddled to the doorway, which he almost filled. 'It's all right, May,' he called. 'I'll be up in a minute.'

'If anything's happened to my girl,' Scanlon said, 'I'll be after you and Walter Loomis and Thomas Kippax and every other fucker responsible. You got that?'

Georges nodded.

Scanlon lifted the cushion on the wet chair to reveal the pistol. He took it, wiped it on the cushion, and put it in his jacket pocket. He also took Georges' cigarettes and lighter. 'And don't tell Trish we're coming.'

'I told you—I don't know her number.'

'I believe you, Edgar. I believe you.'

Georges watched at the window until the Laser pulled away from the kerb. It seemed to take an age to do so. Then he went up to the first landing on the stairs and told his wife that he wasn't well and would stay up for a while. The brandy and scotch decanters had been smashed. He poured vodka over ice and took a long drink before picking up the phone and dialling Kippax's number.

'He was here. I told him,' Georges said.

Kippax said, 'Good. His mood?'

'Aggressive.'

'To be expected.'

'He smashed up my bar.'

'You've been more than compensated over the years. Anything further?'

'Yes. He's got that WPU bloke with him—Dunlop, he calls himself. You'd better tell Trish it's not going to be easy. I think I might ... take a bit of leave for a while.'

'Good idea,' Kippax said. 'Goodnight.'

Georges held the dead phone in his hand for a long time before replacing it. *You cold cunt*, he thought. He was fairly sure that he knew what Scanlon had on Kippax—the killing of his brother. But Georges had no details and certainly no proof. He was glad of the fact. He drank some more vodka and became aware of the wet pyjamas clinging to him. He surveyed the damage to his bar and favourite chair and contemplated the loss of his pistol. Dave Scanlon had taken all the points. Well, the pyjamas could be washed, the mess could be cleaned up and the chair replaced. With crusading independent politicians, the SCCA and witness protection programs, the game was getting tricky. Edgar Georges began to think of accelerating his retirement to Horse Bay.

'Tough stuff,' Dunlop said when they were back in the car.

Scanlon lit a Rothman's, drew deeply and blew the smoke out the open window. He coughed and inhaled again. 'He's a gutless wonder, always was. A pretty good bagman, though. I'll give him that.'

Dunlop started the car. 'D'you think you could shoot someone in cold blood?'

'I don't know,' Scanlon said. 'We'll just have to wait and see, won't we? What I can't figure is why you're going along with all this so quietly. You're supposed to be a hot-shot at this protection stuff. What've you got up your sleeve?'

'Fuck all. You don't need any protecting at the moment. People might need protecting from you. I'd have done something if you'd let go with the sawn-off.'

'I wanted to.'

'I could see that. But you just broke some glass and spilled a bit of booze like any pissed-off hoon in a pub.'

'Drive.' Scanlon coughed violently and fought for breath. He swore, spat phlegm and threw the cigarette out into the gutter. 'We're going to Belle-vue Hill.'

Dunlop moved away and saw the curtain in Georges' window flicker as he did so. 'From what you tell me, Trish's going to be a tougher proposition than Edgar. What're you going to do?'

'Get Mirabelle back.'

Dunlop shook his head. 'Come on, Dave, use your head. If she's in this really deep she'll have worked out something to stop you doing that.'

'Like what?'

'I can think of a dozen ways to freak out a concerned father—an item of clothing, a bit of hair, a polaroid.'

'If I can get close to her...'

'Unlikely. I think you've lost it a bit, mate.'

'What the fuck do you mean?'

Dunlop drove a considerable distance before he answered. The late night traffic was light, easy to handle and he seemed to be getting a kind of second wind. He felt physically tired but mentally sharp. He knew from experience that it was a treacherous condition that could quickly reverse itself or result in complete fatigue. 'It's too pat,' he said. 'Edgar was scared all right, but he wasn't just scared of you. When he gave you the address he was relieved, glad to be getting rid of it. I've seen it before.'

'Fuck,' Scanlon said. 'You think she knows we're coming?'

'That's my guess. What will you do, Dave?'

'Negotiate.'

'I hope so,' Dunlop said.

15

Trish Tillotson was wearing tight jeans and a red silk shirt. She had showered and renewed her make-up. Unknown to Phillip, she had taken two amphetamine capsules—one quick acting, the other slow release—and she was feeling fresh and ready. She hung up the phone and took a pistol and a disposable syringe from a drawer.

'They're coming,' she said as she stripped the wrapping from the syringe.

'What ... what's that for?'

'The needle's to remind Dave of what can happen to little girls who get into bad company. The gun's because he'll have one for sure.'

Phillip was dressed and had washed his hands and face and combed his hair. The brandy-laced coffee had picked him up momentarily, but he could feel the energy already beginning to drain away. He stared at Trish's thin, tight rump and the shape of her legs above the medium-heel shoes. Everything about her excited him, even the syringe and the gun, although he couldn't get rid of the feeling that they were stage props, not real. The sharp click as she checked the mechanism, slotted home the magazine, dispelled that illusion, but he still couldn't believe he was a participant in this bizarre event.

'What... what are we going to do?'

Trish crossed the room, bent down and kissed him. 'You're not going to do anything. You're not going to be here. Go down to the garage and wait. Here's the key and the torch.'

'The garage. But...'

'I can handle it. Believe me. There's nothing to worry about. And Phillip...'

'Yes?'

'You don't need to have any thoughts about protecting me. It just isn't like that. Do you understand?'

'But what if...?'

'There's no if. In an hour or so they'll be gone and I'll come and get you. Then we can fuck again if you want to. Get going, darling!'

Phillip pulled on his jacket and left quickly, surprised to find his legs a little shaky on the steps. His back was sore too, and he knew why. He grinned as he opened the garage door and slipped inside. He shone the torch around but avoided playing the beam on the boxes. He opened the Saab's passenger side door and sat down. He adjusted the seat, pushing it back and altering the rake so that he could stretch his legs and recline comfortably. He found he was able to forget about the dead girl *and* her dangerous father *and* the whole bizarre business. His mind went blank for several minutes and he was suddenly alarmed when he realised that this had happened. For years his habit had been to analyse and assess, evaluate and decide, and here he was thinking nothing and leaving all the decisions to a woman he'd met a bare few hours before. *Am I having a nervous breakdown?*

125

He fought down the panic, let his head rest against the padded seat and closed his eyes. He was asleep almost at once and was soon dreaming about Trish and Thomas Kippax. They were having a meeting at which he was present but unable to make a contribution. Each time he tried to speak Trish opened her blouse and showed him her breasts while Kippax wrote a cheque and threw it at him. The cheques accumulated in front of him and he was rampantly erect, but unable to speak or move. The dream faded and then he was driving his car along a pier that stretched away into the distance. Trish was beside him, shining a torch out onto the boats tied up on either side. The tyres bumped on loose boards and the sails flapped on the yachts and Trish told him to drive faster...

'How smart are you feeling, Luke?' Scanlon said as the Laser turned into Hickson Street.

'Not very,' Dunlop said. 'If she knows we're coming she must reckon she holds all the cards. Have you got any idea of how to get an edge on her?'

'No. She's a murderous bitch is all I know. What worries me is I might do my nut when I see her.'

Dunlop went past the block of flats—quiet, respectable-looking, ample parking in the driveway, pleasant, professionally tended garden. He turned at the end of the street and came back slowly, watching for movement, oddly situated cars, unaccountable-for lights.

'I could do the talking, but it's you she'll want to see. You know the best way to stop yourself from doing anything silly, don't you?'

'Yeah.' Scanlon's foot prodded the overnight bag. 'Leave it behind.'

'And the piece you took from Georges.'

'No way. That's insurance against you, nothing else.'

They left the car and walked up the driveway, inspecting the flats carefully. Several lights were burning and there was music playing softly from a second-floor balcony. Scanlon pointed at an entrance with several flat numbers etched into the glass beside the doorway. Dunlop nodded. He took a set of pick-locks from his pocket and set to work on the security door.

'Illegal,' Scanlon said.

The lock gave and Dunlop hissed with satisfaction. 'After a while in this game, you forget what legal means.'

Scanlon grunted, hit the time-lapse light switch, and went ahead of Dunlop who hung back, watching for watchers. When he was satisfied, he followed Scanlon up the stairs. There was no sound from the ground-level flats or from the others that shared the first landing with Flat 4. The light went out and Scanlon pressed the switch. He examined the door, noting the hinges encased in tempered steel and the recessed lock.

'Lousy security downstairs but pretty good up here,' he said. 'I'll bet that door's more metal than wood.'

'That'd be my choice,' Dunlop said. 'If I was in her line of work.'

'I was never much good at this bit,' Scanlon said. He kicked at the door, his Reebok sneakers making a dull, drumming sound on the unyielding surface.

Scanlon and Dunlop looked up automatically as a voice came through the intercom mounted above the door. 'I can see you, Dave. Christ, you can't imagine how fucking ugly you look through this lens. That gut's an eyesore.'

Instinctively, Dunlop moved to his right, into the shadows.

Trish's laugh crackled through the intercom. 'It's a wide-angle lens, arsehole. I can see the whole landing. You want to talk to me, Dave, or fuck me? Done a bit of both in the past, haven't we?'

'I wouldn't fuck you if you had the last cunt open,' Scanlon said. 'Where's my daughter?'

'So we know where we stand. We'd better talk. Take all your clothes off, both of you.'

Scanlon's jaw dropped. 'What?'

'If you and fucking Carter-Dunlop there want to come in and talk to me you're going to have to do it in the buff. I know you'll have a gun, Dave. You can stick it up your arse if you like. I'll take the chance.'

'Trish...'

'No chat, Dave. This is non-negotiable.'

Scanlon glanced at Dunlop, who shrugged. He was intrigued by the harsh voice with its acquired, cultivated accent. As a professional in dealing with threatening situations, he recognised the expertise and experience behind Trish Tillotson's proposal. Naked meant vulnerable, vulnerable meant a strong likelihood of losing. But long odds could ease. 'Dave?'

Scanlon bent to unlace his sneakers. He unfastened one shoe and kicked it off. He started on the other, groaned, lost his balance. His arms flailed as he reached for support that wasn't there. He fell heavily and flopped over onto his back.

'No fucking tricks, Dunlop.'

'It's not a trick,' Dunlop said. He crouched beside Scanlon, whose breathing was irregular. The vein was throbbing in his forehead again and he was rigid down his left side. 'He's a sick man. Open up. We've got to get a doctor for him.'

The door opened and Trish stepped out. She held a pistol in one hand and in the other an electronic stun-gun. 'Lie flat,' she said. 'I was a nurse. I'll take a look at him. Move an inch and I'll use this tazer on you till you piss blood. Get down!'

Dunlop flattened himself, pressing his face into the carpet with his head turned towards where Scanlon lay. He saw Trish perform a brisk, efficient-looking examination before straightening up. The pistol was inches from her right hand, grip forward. The stun-gun, held left-handed, had remained pointed at him the whole time. 'Angina, I'd say. Typical. It's a wonder he made it up the fucking stairs. This is just a turn. He'll be okay. Probably should have a bypass pretty soon.'

'You're all heart,' Dunlop mumbled.

Trish patted Scanlon's pockets and found the .38. She skidded it back across the carpet through the open door into the flat. 'Now yours. Gently.'

Dunlop slid his pistol across to her as Scanlon stirred and muttered incoherently.

'All things considered,' Trish said, 'I'll let you keep your clothes on. Haul the old bastard in, if you're strong enough.'

'He needs a doctor.'

'When we finish here you can book him into St Vinny's for all I care. Come in or piss off.'

Scanlon was conscious and struggling to rise.

Dunlop helped him to stagger into the flat, down a short passage and into the living room. He guided him to a chair and Scanlon flopped into it, breathing heavily. Trish appeared, holding her pistol in one hand and a glass of water in the other. Dunlop took the glass and held it for Scanlon to drink. A good deal of it spilled down his sweat-soaked shirt but he drank some, spluttering. Colour returned slowly to his face and his breathing became less laboured. He rubbed his left arm and shoulder with his right hand.

Trish leaned against the wall. 'Crook ticker you've got there, Dave. Too many steak sandwiches and schooners of old. Still on the Chesterfields?'

'Where's Mirabelle?' Scanlon gasped. 'If you've hurt her you'll be sorry you were born.'

'You're a windbag. Why should I want to hurt her?' Trish stared at Dunlop, who was sitting quietly on the arm of Scanlon's chair. *They know she's been hurt*, she thought. She licked at her split lip and felt the swelling where Phillip's passionate, clumsy kissing had bruised her. 'You've been to the boat.'

Dunlop nodded. 'Saw the blood.'

'She's all right. It's nothing serious. She's being looked after.'

'I hope so,' Dunlop said. 'For your sake. So what's the deal here?'

'Pretty simple. I want the evidence for whatever Dave has on Thomas Kippax—in exchange for the girl. Also Dave's agreement to change his tune.'

'That leaves Dave well and truly in the shit. He's facing some serious charges if he does the dirty on the SCCA.'

'That's tough. My heart bleeds for him.'

Scanlon's head turned slightly as he watched first

130

one then the other. His lips were moving as if he was repeating what each one said. Dunlop looked down at him with a worried frown.

'What guarantees does Dave get?'

Trish picked up the syringe from the coffee table. 'No guarantees at all. Just a promise that he never sees the girl again if he doesn't play. He knows what I mean.'

Scanlon launched himself from the chair, or attempted to. When he was younger and stronger his dive would have carried him across the room and his head butt would have broken bones. But the attack was painfully slow and ill-coordinated. Scanlon caught his foot on the rug, lost balance and fell, well short of his target. Trish laughed and pointed the pistol at his head as he looked up.

'You fucking clown. All you arseholes are fucking clowns. Detective Inspector! Fuck, I'm ten times more effective than you and your lot, always was.'

'You boong bitch!'

Trish took one half-step forward and kicked him in the face. The edge of her shoe caught him below the right eye and ripped the flesh from his cheekbone. Scanlon moaned and clutched at his face. Dunlop stood and found himself looking down at the pistol. Trish was standing very straight, but relaxed. The gun was pointed at his chest.

'What've you got, Dave? A tape? Photos?'

Blood dripped from Scanlon's hands as he levered himself up from the floor. He wiped one hand on the rumpled beige rug, cleared his throat and spat more blood onto the floor.

'Video,' he said.

'Video. That's good. That's very good. Give me your mobile number, Dunlop. I'll be in touch.'

Scanlon was sitting up now, the right side of his face torn and bleeding with a purple swelling threatening to close the eye. He looked across at Dunlop, who had resumed his seat. But Dunlop was looking around the room as if studying every detail.

'You can't leave it like that. I want ...'

'I don't give a fuck what you want, Dave. It's what *I* want that counts now. And I want a bit of time to work a few things out.'

'To put the screws on, you mean,' Dunlop said.

Trish laughed. 'You're not altogether dumb, honey. Cute, too. Pity I didn't get you to strip. I bet you'd have looked a hell of a lot better than fat-gut Dave. The number!'

Dunlop recited it.

'Again. Slowly.'

He repeated it.

'Okay. Got it. I'll toss the guns off the balcony. How does it feel to get outsmarted and stood over by a woman, Dave? A first for you, eh? You were a lousy fuck, too. I might as well tell you that.'

16

Dunlop helped Scanlon down the stairs. The two men stood in the garden and watched Trish Tillotson drop their weapons into the flowerbeds. Scanlon rested against a brick pillar while Dunlop retrieved the guns. Music was still flowing from the second-floor balcony, but there were no other sounds or noises from the flats. The block was a quiet island in a quiet sea. Dunlop looked at the cars parked in the driveway.

'What does she drive?' he asked.

Scanlon's face was pale in the dim light. His jowls sagged and his weatherbeaten skin looked ready to peel away. 'She doesn't fucking drive. Hates it. Why?'

'Nothing. You're not looking the best, Dave. Come on back to the car. I don't want you having another turn on me.'

'We have to talk about…'

'Yeah. In a minute. I think I've got a flask of brandy there. Might steady you down. Come on.'

He supported Scanlon as they moved slowly up the driveway to the street. The big man's weight was telling on him by the time he reached the top and he realised that he'd have had difficulty in making the walk unaided. He took a breather and half-dragged an apologetic Scanlon to the car. He found the brandy in the glove box and put the bottle in Scanlon's hands. 'Only an inch or so. Take it slowly. Be back in a minute.'

Scanlon's head lolled. 'Where you going?'

'Just hang on.'

'Hope I get a chance to put one in her.'

'Sure, Dave.'

Dunlop jogged back towards the flats, ducking into the shadows and moving down the driveway under the cover of the parked cars. He was tired and jangle-nerved, but alerted by what he'd noticed. Several of the cars were dark and several were foreign—a Mercedes, a Volvo, an Alfa Romeo—but none was dark *and* foreign. There were three roller-door garages at the rear of the block. Dunlop worked his way towards them, pressing himself back against the ivy-covered brick wall that divided the flats from a high-rise apartment block at the rear. He squinted—the white paint had faded, but the three doors had 4, 8 and 12 stencilled on them. Dunlop looked up at the block—there were three corner flats offering larger balconies than the rest with 180-degree views. Trish Tillotson's and two others. With car spaces.

Trish came walking briskly towards the garages. The area was poorly lit but she was sure-footed, confident of avoiding obstacles. She was almost sprightly, walking with exaggerated energy. *High on some bloody thing,* Dunlop thought. He watched as she knocked on the door marked 4. The consternation she displayed when she got no response was the

134

first sign of discomposure Dunlop had seen in her. He was glad to see it. *What's the matter, Trishy? Lost something?*

She bent, took hold of the door handle and lifted. The door rolled up smoothly and quietly and she stepped into the darkness. Dunlop heard a metallic click and a faint light showed inside the garage. He heard murmured voices, saw a stronger light and then the quiet closing of a car door. Trish emerged with her arm around a tall, fair-headed man. *Biggish bloke… pretty fit.* Except that he was looking about as tired as Dunlop felt. Trish closed and locked the garage door and the pair walked hand-in-hand out of the range of Dunlop's vision. Trish held a torch and flicked the beam around the area in front of the garage. Dunlop held his breath as the light danced towards him, but it wasn't strong enough to reach his hiding place.

He left the wall and approached the garages. A metal sign bolted between two of the doors advised that armed guards of Eastern Suburbs Security Ltd patrolled the premises. Dunlop used his pick-locks on the door and had it open and raised in less than two minutes. He went in and discerned the shape of the motor car occupying the space. He closed the garage door before trying the driver's door. It opened and the car's interior light came on. Dunlop noted that the back doors were unlocked. He studied the back seat and felt around on the upholstery and panelling. His hand touched something that had dried onto the carpet, and he picked at it and sniffed. He froze as he heard footsteps approaching. Silently he closed the driver's door, shutting off the light. There was a rattle as the first of the garage doors was tried. The tread was heavy. The second door was shaken. Then the footsteps retreated, the guard evidently having decided that checking two of the three doors was sufficient.

Slack. Dunlop waited until the footsteps had receded before opening the car door again. He was calculating times and distances, wondering whether Trish and her companion would have had time to deposit Mirabelle somewhere before getting to Bellevue Hill. *Hard to say.* The Saab had a commodious boot and Dunlop contemplated forcing it. He turned on the overhead light and cast about for a suitable tool. A large screwdriver lay on top of a double row of tea chests. Dunlop reached for it, slipped on an oily patch and grabbed at the boxes for support. He missed his hold, knocked two of the tea chests down and cut his hand on the tin strapping. He swore and sucked at the cut, bent for the screwdriver and saw the shape, now only half-concealed by the boxes, lying against the wall.

'Oh, Jesus. Oh, no.'

He crawled across the floor, pushing the tea chests aside, and lifted the blanket-wrapped bundle clear. Gently, he uncovered one end and his teeth clicked together painfully as he looked into Mirabelle's wide-open, sightless grey eyes.

'Bastards. You scumbag bastards.'

The girl's head lay at an odd angle in a way that Dunlop, who had attended many road accidents in his police career, instantly recognised. He completed the unwrapping and saw the thigh wound. He rocked back on his heels, his mind flooding with possibilities, explanations, strategies. The result was confusion. *What the fuck am I going to do now?*

136

Despite himself, he couldn't help recognising that the knowledge of Mirabelle's death neutralised any advantage Trish Tillotson thought she enjoyed. But there was no way that David Scanlon could cope with the information in his present condition.

Dunlop worked quickly, restoring the blanket to its previous position, putting the body back against the wall and replacing the boxes and the screwdriver. He closed the door of the Saab, turned off the light and lifted the roller door sufficiently to enable him to get under it in a crouch. He eased the door back down and moved quickly back up the driveway to the street, keeping an eye on the balcony and windows of Flat 4. A reddish light showed at one window, otherwise the flat was in darkness. No sound came from the balcony where the music had been playing. Dunlop reached the street and strode towards the Laser. His leg muscles ached and he realised that his face was set in a rictus of pain and concentration.

'Dave?'

He opened the passenger door and found Scanlon slumped in the seat, tilting forward and sideways towards the steering wheel. His breath was coming in short gasps and the left side of his body appeared to be frozen. His eyes were closed and his jaw was slack, sagging to the left. Dunlop eased Scanlon into a position where the seat would contain him and fastened his seat belt. Scanlon's breathing was tortured but steady and his pulse was fluttering but constant. He got quickly behind the wheel, started the car and punched buttons on his mobile phone.

'Dunlop,' he said when the call was answered. 'Client with heart attack or stroke or both. Coming in at once. Full-scale medical attendance required.'

The private hospital used by the WPU was in Surry Hills. Dunlop battled fatigue as he drove at speed through the quiet streets. The brandy flask rolled around on the floor at Scanlon's feet as Dunlop braked and put the Laser through tight turns. Two images were fixed in his mind. First, the arrogant strut of Trish Tillotson in her red shirt and tight jeans, hand-in-hand with a tall young man, both healthy-looking and fit, sexually linked, walking away. And the concealed, broken body of Mirabelle, scarcely more than a child, and the only thing in the world that mattered to the man sitting next to him.

Dunlop pulled up in front of the hospital and an expert team swung into action. Scanlon was unstrapped, lifted onto a gurney and wheeled up a ramp and through a set of perspex doors. Edgar Georges' packet of Rothman's fell onto the pavement and Dunlop, propped against the car, saw it and was momentarily tempted. He shrugged the impulse away and went in search of coffee.

'Mr Dunlop!'

Dunlop was shaken awake by a nurse who held a styrofoam cup, the same as the other two sitting empty on the arm of the chair where he'd fallen asleep.

'Mr Dunlop, the doctor wants you in the ward.'

Dunlop forced his eyes to open and his brain to engage. The nurse's grip was firm and she shook him solidly. *A big woman, wide-shouldered and fair— nothing like Trish Tillotson*. Dunlop's arm jerked and knocked the empty cups to the floor.

'Careful, please!'

'Sorry. Sorry. Where should I go?'

'Second floor. I think you should drink this first and freshen up. The men's toilet is beside the lift.'

Dunlop took the cup and sipped. The coffee was hot but his tastebuds had ceased working. He couldn't tell whether it was heavily sugared as the other two cups had been or not. His mouth was a sour cavern. 'Thank you, nurse. Can you tell me...'

'It's sister, if you don't mind, and I'm afraid I can't tell you anything. You'll have to talk to doctor.'

Dunlop said 'Thank you' again and struggled to his feet. He collected the empty cups and dropped them in a bin. After a long swallow from the full cup it followed the others. He washed his face in the men's room, rinsed his mouth several times and ran his fingers through his hair which had become greasy and lank in the course of the day. He stared at himself in the mirror, thinking that he looked only marginally better than Dave Scanlon when he'd last seen him. He rode the lift to the second floor, where he was met by a bespectacled, white-coated doctor who introduced himself as Peter Mockridge.

'Your man's in a bad way, I'm afraid,' Mockridge said. 'I don't honestly think he can last the night.'

Dunlop blinked. 'Come on, haven't you got life-support systems and all that?'

'That's only suitable for some cases. Mr Scanlon's got a multiplicity of problems. Very significant occlusions, of course, but that's complicated by an arrhythmic problem and a serious thrombotic condition. He needs a multiple bypass and a pacemaker, but he's in no condition to survive the surgery. He's got emphysema and he's vulnerable to pneumonia just from the sedation he's had so far to relieve the hysteria he went into. I'm sorry, Mr Dunlop, but he's a write-off.'

'So what are you telling me?'

'As I say, he's unlikely to make it through the night. There's at least three things poised to kill him, so if you want to talk to him, you'd better do it right away.'

'He's lucid?'

'For now.'

Dunlop followed the doctor down the corridor to the room where Scanlon lay on a narrow bed. A tube ran from his nose and several others snaking from his left arm were connected to a stand beside the bed and an electronic device mounted at its foot. Dunlop threaded his way through the apparatus and bent over Scanlon, whose breathing was still shallow, although less laboured. His eyes were closed.

'Dave, it's Dunlop.'

Scanlon's eyes opened and showed no comprehension before closing again.

Dunlop glanced at Mockridge, who shrugged. 'It's Frank Carter, Dave,' he said. 'Uniform from Five Dock, plain clothes at the Cross. You remember me.'

The eyes flickered. 'Golf.'

'That's right, Dave. We played golf today—you and me. Three and three and two halves.'

'Mirabelle,' Scanlon said.

'Yes, Dave. We'll find her. Where's the video? Where's the Kippax video?'

The voice was a faint whisper. 'Mirabelle.'

'Dave—where's the video?'

'Mirabelle.'

'Dave...'

Scanlon sucked in air painfully as if his body was

140

reluctant to take it. He twitched and gasped. The blue vein in his forehead pulsed.

'Doctor!'

Mockridge threw open the door and bellowed for a nurse. He almost threw himself on Scanlon, pummelling his flabby chest and thumping his rib cage. A nurse rushed into the room and Mockridge spewed words at her that Dunlop did not understand. He stood uselessly at the bedside while Mockridge massaged and pounded. The nurse returned carrying a loaded syringe with a long needle. Mockridge ripped aside the hospital gown and plunged the needle into Scanlon's chest in a way that almost caused Dunlop to throw up.

'Lift his arms,' Mockridge barked.

Dunlop and the nurse raised the limp arms, pumped them up and down while Mockridge withdrew the needle and looked anxiously at the electronic monitor. Dunlop shot the screen a glance and saw the flat, unwavering green line.

The nurse was sweating. 'Doctor?'

Dunlop saw that the fat vein in Scanlon's sunblasted forehead had ceased throbbing. He pumped the arm again, but it felt like trying to draw water from a dry well.

Mockridge was sweating almost as much as the nurse. He tore his eyes from the screen and looked at Dunlop. 'I'm sorry,' he said. 'He's gone.'

PART II

17

'It's difficult to see how you could have handled things more ineptly,' Burton said.

Dunlop sat, turning an envelope in his hands, and said nothing. He'd been unable to sleep since taking Scanlon to hospital. Completely unable. Hours of report writing and question-and-answer sessions hadn't tired him. His nerves were shot from too much coffee. Whisky hadn't helped, nor had pills or hot baths. He felt he'd become the world expert at staring at blank walls.

'Scanlon dead, his daughter missing. Wild accusations from you with absolutely no proof and this disgraceful story.'

Burton pushed a newspaper across the table towards Dunlop, who ignored it. The headline read: MINDERS HAVE SEX WHILE GIRL VANISHES. The story, sourced to 'a person within the Witness Protection Unit', alleged that two senior officers slept together and neglected security at a safe house from which Mirabelle Scanlon had disappeared.

Burton retrieved the paper and read, his voice dripping with sarcasm. '"*Mirabelle, attractive 16-year-old daughter of former detective Dave 'Sailor'*

Scanlon, is still missing following the death of her father two days ago. The ex-policeman was due to give evidence to an SCCA hearing on stock market manipulation and other high-level white collar crime, but died of a massive heart attack the day before the inquiry opened. The senior member of the protection team allegedly played golf with Scanlon…" Golf, Jesus, you must have been out of your mind.'

'It was his idea,' Dunlop said sullenly. 'I was just keeping him happy, as per orders. The story's bullshit—no-one ever called Dave Scanlon "Sailor" in his life.'

'Flip comments won't help. This is a monumental cock-up. I notice you don't deny the accuracy of the report in one respect.'

Dunlop shrugged. 'The timing's all to shit. It was the night before—it had nothing to do with the girl getting loose. I've told you—this is Lucy Scanlon's work. She hated Dave and the girl. She was a plant. She kept Tillotson or Kippax or both informed of what was going on. That's how they got to the girl before we did.'

'That's absurd. Mrs Scanlon has been too distraught to make any comment at all.'

Dunlop's laugh was a short, harsh bark. 'Dream on, *Mr* Burton. Believe what you like.'

'Your attitude is not helpful. Miss Hardy has been reprimanded and re-assigned. She has taken her medicine and will have to abide by the consequences. I am persuaded that the real negligence here is yours. Tadros wounded, Scanlon dead…'

'Don't forget the dog, Rusty, with his throat cut. That's got to be my fault too. Oh yes, and the girl— broken neck, fucking great wound in her leg…'

'That garage was gone over, inch by inch…'

'You just can't grasp it, can you? Trish Tillotson's an expert. She'd be three jumps ahead of you on one of her slow days. She knows how to protect a scene-of-crime site and how to make it look like there's been a kid's picnic there with balloons and chocolate crackles.'

Burton looked down at his notes. 'You say there was a Saab sedan in the garage, but you didn't even get the number.'

'There was a lot happening and I wasn't fucking-well taking notes. I read the number and tried to remember it, but I'd just found a dead girl and then her father was terminating in my car. I'll admit to that deficiency—I fucking forgot it!'

'You should have…'

Dunlop's control snapped. 'Don't fucking tell me what I should have fucking done! You weren't there. Your kind's never there. I had Sammy Tadros down and… has anyone talked to Edgar Georges?'

'He's gone on leave, and don't even bother to ask about Thomas Kippax. I've read your statement. It's the most complete can of worms I've ever seen and no-one wants to open it.'

Dunlop sneered. 'That'd be right. Pick away at the mozzie bites and ignore the fucking shark that's going to swallow you alive. This discreet little inquiry you've been conducting is a farce. It's all bullshit. Trish Tillotson murdered the girl, or helped her on her way and no-one's even going to ask her a question or two.'

'She's…'

'Got high-level protection. I know.'

'I was going to say that she's a senior officer with an impressive service record.'

'She's a cold-blooded murderous bitch, corrupt from head to toe.'

Burton shuffled papers uneasily. 'Can't you see the way things stand? You're levelling accusations at a respectable business figure, a grieving widow, senior police, while you yourself are under a cloud for negligence and inefficiency.'

'Why am I here, then?'

'I hope to persuade you to undergo a psychological evaluation. It's a stressful role, the one you've been fulfilling for some time now with distinction. This is for your protection. It can secure you generous sick or retirement benefits...'

'No way.'

'I'm sorry. Observations have been made and your conduct has been deemed erratic to put it mildly. Look at you, you're twitching as you sit there. You're skin and bone. When did you last sleep?'

'Fuck you.'

'You're irrational, ignoring your own best interests. A suspension is the very least you can expect.'

'No, it's not.' Dunlop tossed the envelope onto the polished surface. It skidded across and teetered on the edge, almost falling into Burton's lap. 'I resign.'

'A video?' Thomas Kippax was sceptical. 'What the hell do you mean, a video? Of what?'

Trish Tillotson, sitting alongside Phillip Krabbe, both in Kippax's commodious leather office chairs, shrugged. 'I don't know. That's all he said.'

Kippax moved things around on his desk with

impatient hands. He had been reluctant to meet with the policewoman again after hearing of Scanlon's death, but Phillip Krabbe, uncharacteristically, had insisted.

'I'd say you were getting well beyond your brief,' Kippax said. 'Requiring him to produce evidence.'

'My brief was never very clear, Mr Kippax,' Phillip interposed smoothly. The events and emotions of the past few days had produced remarkable changes in him. He no longer had a sleek, self-satisfied look. Worry and exertion had stripped flesh from him; excitement—sexual, physical and mental—had raised the tempo of his metabolism and existence. He spoke more quickly than before and let fewer words do more work. 'It was necessary to press Scanlon. Detective Tillotson was right in taking the initiative.'

Sex finished well behind the pursuit and exercise of power as a motif in Thomas Kippax's life, but he had experienced it enough, and most recently and satisfyingly with Lucy Scanlon, to appreciate its power and recognise the signs of it at work. *He's screwing her*, he thought. *Or rather, she's screwing him.* The thought of playing the unholy matchmaker would have amused him if there had not been so much at stake. With his new perception of Krabbe and Tillotson as allies, the dynamics of the meeting had subtly changed and not, in his instinctive judgement, for the better.

Kippax mentally reproached himself for having shown antagonism, and affected a world-weary air, 'Scanlon could well have been lying, you know. Trying to buy time, contrive a situation more advantageous to himself. It sounds as if you'd given him very little room in which to manoeuvre.'

149

'If that's meant as a criticism, its misjudged,' Phillip said. 'We secured the first objective—preventing Scanlon from testifying. The point about the evidence was a logical...'

Trish longed to touch him—his arm, his knee, any part. Despite herself, she'd become obsessed by him in a way that she'd seen in other women and always despised. Her motto—that a cock was six inches long, more or less, and it didn't matter what other meat it was attached to—was failing her. She shifted in her seat and crossed her legs. The movement caught Phillip's eye and he stopped talking.

'I made one mistake,' Trish said quickly. 'I should have seen that he was desperately sick—dying, in fact. Those old coppers are like that—all fat guts and high colour and short breath. But the signs were there. I should have shown him the girl's knickers or something, and got it all out of him there and then.'

Kippax was the son of a wealthy man and he had fallen heir to all the advantages of his class—education, influential connections, travel. But he knew plenty of men who had enjoyed the same privileges and fallen by the wayside in the post-regulatory business world. He hadn't expanded and diversified his assets by being unobservant and uncritical. He sensed that Tillotson and Krabbe, although deferential enough now, were playing a different game. Blackmail, almost certainly. And not about the Scanlon girl. They were too vulnerable there themselves. The other thing, then. When would he ever be clear of it?

'Look, Detective Tillotson... Trish. I'm not undervaluing your efforts. Stopping Scanlon was the first objective, as Phillip rightly says. And that was achieved most satisfactorily.'

Trish nodded, accepting the olive branch.

Kippax willed himself to relax further. He abandoned the items he'd been fidgeting with and laid his hands squarely on the desk. 'It's possible that the pressure you subjected him to put him over the edge. What's the matter, Phillip? I hope you're not getting squeamish at this stage?'

Kippax had noted Krabbe's discomfiture. He had winced and glanced, agitatedly, around the room as the policewoman's name had been spoken. Kippax let out a laugh that was almost hearty. 'You must not concern yourself. This room is swept for surveillance devices almost hourly. The whole level is clear, although I wouldn't vouch for the rest of the building.'

'Are you sure you can trust your own people, Thomas?' Trish Tillotson asked.

A great team, Kippax thought. *Backing each other up.* His mind ran back over several meetings with Scanlon and others at the time when he was pressing his brother, Louis, for control of the Kippax media group. It was some years back when video camera technology was less well developed, but it was just possible. It represented a threat he had not anticipated. Allegations from Scanlon, notes, diaries, were one thing, but recorded evidence was quite another. The danger had to be considered. The question was, how to do it without nurturing another, and perhaps worse, threat?

'We have a problem,' Kippax barked suddenly. 'What's the key to the solution?'

'Edgar Georges and Dunlop,' Trish said. 'Look at it this way—Scanlon was lying or he told no-one. In either event, no problem. If he put the

151

video somewhere utterly safe that only he knew about, it's unlikely to turn up, ever. There's a chance, though, that he'd told Dunlop and I think Edgar Georges knows a lot more about this than he's let on.'

Kippax stopped her with an upraised finger. 'If you're right about Dunlop, then that's the end of it. The evidence will come to light.'

Trish shook her head. 'Not necessarily. My information is that the WPU bigwigs are rousting Dunlop for incompetence and negligence. They're really pissed off with him. You've seen the newspaper articles?'

Kippax nodded.

'Added to that, Dunlop's a maverick of sorts. There's no telling what he'll do. I propose that Phillip get in touch with him, sound him out, see how the land lies. Stall things, possibly.'

'Agreed,' Kippax said. 'But with regard to Georges—what's your thinking there?'

'We know Dunlop and Scanlon went to see Edgar before he came to my place. We also know that they went there to get my address. But what else happened? What else did they talk about? Why has Edgar shot through? I'd like to know.'

Kippax's antennae fluttered and his mind raced. *She's lying through her teeth. She's got something else altogether in mind.* He knew now where his greatest danger lay and it was ironical that she just might have provided the remedy. He frowned, miming serious consideration of the proposition. 'You could be right, of course. You seem to have every contingency covered. What's the problem here?'

'I don't know where Edgar's gone.'

Phillip recalled how Trish had sprung into action

152

when she'd learned of Scanlon's death. Her energy had seemed endless and he'd had to drive himself to the limit to keep up with her. He shied away from remembering the place where they'd taken the body. He could scarcely believe that she'd had the capacity to plan a strategy involving Dunlop and organise helpers. But she had. He had difficulty in concealing his admiration, but he kept to the agreed script. 'You didn't tell me about this.'

Kippax noted Krabbe's reaction. *So they're not totally hand-in-glove*, he reflected. *That's something.* He excused himself and tapped a button on his console and took a phone call, willing to observe the pair in dialogue and possible conflict. The call was routine, requiring a minimal amount of his attention. In other circumstances, he would have found the policewoman attractive himself—dark, rail-thin, dressed conservatively in white blouse and dark skirt, but giving the clothes a provocative note with ankle-strapped high heeled shoes and a black ribbon around the straight, slender column of her neck. Krabbe was obviously captivated to beyond his wit's end, Kippax concluded. The woman was in a state of near-rut, too, but no less dangerous for it. The phone call had absorbed none of his attention. He had the solution. 'I can tell you where he is. Tasmania. And I can give you some details. But please, be very, very discreet about going there and reporting back.'

'Thank you, Thomas.' Trish stood and moved towards the door.

Phillip Krabbe held his ground, showing no interest in her graceful movement. At no time had the question of Mirabelle Scanlon's whereabouts been discussed, but Phillip was becoming used to dealings in which the crucial subject went unmentioned. Now, he was acting under Trish's orders again. He advanced to the desk and extended his hand.

'Thank you, Mr Kippax. It's been a pleasure to meet you and I'm sure everything will work out well.'

Kippax shook hands, an action he disliked but had learned to tolerate. 'I trust so.'

In the private elevator that led from Kippax's office suite to a lower floor, Trish and Phillip embraced and kissed passionately.

'We're probably being filmed and bugged,' Phillip said.

'Who cares?'

Nevertheless, they waited until they were in Phillip's car before getting down to business.

'I picked up a definite reaction,' Trish said. 'To Edgar Georges. Did you notice how quick he was to tell me where Edgar is? He'd sell his own mother, that man. What about his hands?'

'Damp,' Phillip said. 'Decidedly damp. Do you think he knows about us?'

'Yes, and it bothers him. Thomas likes to control everything and everybody. He can feel this one slipping away from him and he doesn't like it. We're close to getting him by the balls.'

'We need the video.'

'Not necessarily. We could get by with knowing what's on it and by being sure that no-one else has it. Thomas's wide open to a very big bluff. He's falling for small ones already.'

Phillip swerved skilfully to avoid a motorcyclist. Since meeting Trish it was only while driving that he felt in control of anything. He didn't care. 'I can't keep up with you. What d'you mean?'

Trish laughed. 'You're not going to tackle Dunlop. Thomas was right the first time. If he's got the evidence then the game's over. I don't think he has got it. I'm still not sure it even exists. But Thomas is seriously worried about Georges. So we're going to have a little trip, just you and me, lover. We're off to Tassie for a talk with fat Edgar.'

18

Dunlop's first thought on leaving the WPU building was to get drunk. Then the American saying jumped into his head: Don't get mad, get even.

'Don't get drunk, get even,' he said aloud in the street and laughed.

Several people turned to look at him. An Aboriginal youth washing a shop window stopped whistling and grinned at him. 'Get drunk *and* get even,' he said. 'But better get even first.'

'Yeah,' Dunlop said. 'Thanks.'

Burton hadn't taken his gesture seriously, hadn't asked for the surrender of his credentials or equipment. Indeed, Dunlop was not sure that he *could* terminate his employment simply with a letter of resignation. He recalled the forms he'd signed and undertakings he'd made when he'd joined the unit. Disengagement was likely to be at least as formal and paper-bound. But he considered himself free of official restraints and proposed to use the freedom.

Maddy had told him of Lucy Scanlon's collapse on getting the news of her husband's death. She'd ceased to be a WPU client at that point and had returned to the Randwick house, where Russell and Geoff had been re-employed to keep the media at bay. He didn't anticipate any serious trouble from Russell or Geoff.

Dunlop drove to Randwick under a dark, purplish sky. A storm was gathering in the west, threatening to sweep over the city and expend its energy out to sea, or hit with full force within the next hour. He switched on the radio for a weather report and heard nothing that his eyes hadn't already revealed. People were putting up shutters; shopkeepers were checking their awnings and pulling display boards inside. Electricity crackled in the air and interfered with the radio reception. Dunlop switched off and concentrated on his driving. The wind that had been blowing all morning, and had contributed to his feeling of alienation and disenchantment, had dropped. The streetside trees were still with stiff leaves, as if braced for what was to come.

Dunlop turned into Carrington Road and, from long habit, went past the house, turned and came back. He wondered how long it would be before he'd be able to pull up outside a house without subjecting it to a wary scrutiny. Perhaps never. His resentment against the whole law enforcement culture was building. He was aware of it, but powerless to defuse it. He sat in the car, looking at the house—a temple of police corruption, with its over-elaborate security gates and florid architecture—and thought about what his life in the police world had cost him. A marriage, his very name and identity, several relationships that might have been successful in a different context. By the time he reached the gate, Frank Carter, a.k.a. Lucas Dunlop, was a very angry man.

Geoff ran his hand over his blonded brushcut and sneered through the grille. 'Big help you were.'

157

'I want to see Lucy.'

'Forget it. She's distraught. Not seeing anyone. She's lost her husband and her daughter. Can't you understand that, arsehole?'

Dunlop's hand shot through the gap between the bars. He grabbed Geoff's left hand and pulled it towards him, bending it down and sideways until the forearm lay across a horizontal metal strut while the wrist was braced vertically. 'I hate to think what a good yank would do to your arm, Geoff,' Dunlop said. 'It'd be a long time before you could pump any iron. Maybe never. Shit, we're looking at a transverse ligament and muscle tear. Very nasty.'

Geoff's sunlamp tan faded; he eased back to reduce the pressure. 'What, what d'you want?'

'What I said—to talk to the lady. Press the button and open the gate. Do it easy, or I promise you'll be lifting with the right arm only.'

An electronic whirr sounded and the gate swung in slowly. Dunlop went with it, keeping the pressure on the arm until he could slip through the gap. He released as soon as he was inside and was ready for the savage right-hand karate chop Geoff aimed at his neck. He ducked under it and drove the heel of his hand up into Geoff's nose. He felt exultation as the bone and tissue gave way under the force and timing of the blow. He grabbed the gate in his right hand and swung it into Geoff's dipping head, catching him hard just above the hairline. Blood spurted and Geoff groaned as he went limp. Dunlop took no chances on the feigned collapse stratagem. He brought his knee up sharply and heard the jawbone click out and several teeth splinter as Geoff's head met it coming down.

Dunlop bent and took hold of Geoff's left ear, twisting it up, almost lifting the man from the ground as he spoke. 'I want to be sure you hear this. One, don't be around when I come out. Two, where's Russell?'

Geoff mumbled and red froth fell from his askew mouth. He choked and coughed, yelling with pain as Dunlop kept the grip on his ear. He pointed at the house.

Dunlop let him go and crunched up the gravel driveway, turning off it to follow the cement path to the steps leading to the wide porch at the front of the house. Weeds were threatening to encroach on the path. The porch had a waist-high balustrade with fluted pillars and a tiled surface. The tiles were dull, filmed with dust, and several near the door were scratched. The screen door was locked. Dunlop took out a Swiss army knife, slit the wire and unlatched the door. He pressed the bell and waited. Heavy footsteps muted by thick carpet. The door swung back and Russell stood in the opening, obviously expecting the protection of the screen.

Dunlop's pistol came up so that it was only a few centimetres from the point of Russell's square jaw.

'Your employment is suspended,' Dunlop said. 'Go down there and help your mate. I want to talk to Lucy for a bit. If you behave yourself, I'll let you get back to camera-breaking and that. Where is she?'

Russell bunched a large fist. Dunlop brought the pistol down on it in a hard, whipping motion that split the skin over the knuckles. 'Don't,' he said. 'I'm not in the mood. Where is she?'

Russell looked at the blood seeping from his lacerated knuckles. 'Upstairs, and she'll eat you alive, Dunlop.'

Taking the carpeted stairs three at a time, Dunlop went up to the first-floor landing, where he found Lucy Scanlon leaning over the rail. She wore pink silk lounging pyjamas and white satin slippers. The auburn hair, previously so carefully arranged, hung loosely around her head, but her make-up was immaculate. She held a glass in her hand and was slightly drunk. 'And just what was the point of that brutal display?' she said.

'That was gentle.'

'Oh, I saw what you did at the gate as well. Quite the Rambo, aren't you, Mr Dunlop? When you're not losing people and getting them killed.'

Dunlop studied her closely. On their previous meetings, he had found her self-centred and brittle, but with a calmness to her that suggested a plan or a purpose. Now, she had a lost, embittered look. Perhaps hating Dave and resenting Mirabelle had given her a focus. A thunderclap shook the house and the window above their heads was suddenly lit up by a huge, ragged sheet of lightning ripping across the dark sky. Lucy Scanlon screamed and lurched forward, losing her balance and dropping her glass. Wine spilled over Dunlop's pants as he reached out to prevent her falling. His hands touched the smooth silk and felt the softness of the flesh underneath it. She whimpered and clung to him as the thunder roared again and lightning flared. A gust of wind shook the window and rain hammered against the glass.

Dunlop gently disengaged himself, picked up the glass and kept a hand lightly on the woman's back as they walked from the landing. She was trembling and stumbled once or twice, so that Dunlop had to support her. They went into a large, femininely decorated bedroom with a sunroom and a wall-length set of walk-in closets with mirrored doors. A bottle of white wine sat on a table in the sunroom and she gestured at it. 'I'd like a drink, please. I can't stand these Sydney storms. They really upset me. I remember... Please, have a drink yourself, Mr Dunlop. I'm sorry I was so antagonistic. I really don't know what's happening to me, or what's going to happen.'

A bar fridge stood in the corner of the sunroom. Above it was a wine rack and a shelf holding different-sized crystal goblets. Dunlop filled two glasses with wine and handed one to Lucy Scanlon, who was standing by the window watching the rain lash down on the front garden.

'Thank you. You see, I really did have a very good view of your rather remarkable entrance.'

Dunlop realised that he was able to see directly over her head. In the flat-heeled slippers she would have stood barely 160 centimetres tall. Like the dress she had worn the first time he had seen her, the top of her pyjamas was slightly padded at the shoulder, and he became aware of her smallness. The body inside the loose pink silk was tiny. He looked at the top of her head and saw the dark roots of her hair. She turned to look up at him and he saw that what he had taken for elaborate make-up—the thin, arched brows over slanted eyes and the creamy skin—were natural features of her face.

She smiled, her full lips parting to reveal perfect teeth. 'So, you see me for the first time, Mr Dunlop. Your friend David's Chinese bride.'

Dunlop muttered, 'Is that so?' and drank some wine.

'Yes. Australian father, name unknown, and half-Chinese mother. Born in Hong Kong, educated in a convent and a brothel. You can guess in which place I met David, of course.'

'It's no business of mine.'

'Please, sit down. I need to talk. It was impossible with those two, but you, your business is people. You might understand. You came to talk to me, didn't you?'

Dunlop nodded and sat in a padded wicker chair. Lucy Scanlon continued to stand by the window. She drank and put her glass on the table. She wore silver polish on her long, shaped fingernails and several rings on both hands.

'I didn't come to hear the story of your life though,' Dunlop said roughly. 'I wanted to ask you about your relationship with Thomas Kippax. You realise you're partly responsible for Mirabelle's death?'

The hardness was immediately back in Lucy Scanlon's voice and manner. 'You'll have to explain that. I wasn't aware that she was dead.'

'I believe she is. You reported her missing to Kippax or someone close to him from the Sans Souci house on your mobile phone. That information helped two people to locate her. I very much doubt that any trace will ever be found of her.'

'I don't think you could prove any of that.'

'I don't intend to. I just want to know what you think about it. And this—Dave could have died at any time, but what Kippax's people put him through that night was as good as a bullet in the brain. How do you feel about that, Mrs Scanlon?'

'I've no doubt of it. I'm sure I have a different perspective on such things from you. Have you ever been to Hong Kong, Mr Dunlop?'

162

Dunlop nodded.

'The nicer parts, no doubt. The Peninsula Hotel, perhaps—on a police junket?'

'Not quite that flash, but you're right. I've only been there as a tourist. What's your point?'

'There are much less nice parts of the city, I can tell you, where life is much less pleasant. I spent some time in those places. My mother spent most of her life in them. David promised to bring my mother to Australia when our first child was born. It was a kind of pre-nuptial agreement, if you follow me.'

The storm was passing. There had been only distant rumblings of thunder and the lightning flashes were small and localised. Dunlop finished his wine and wanted more, but he sat quietly. Lucy Scanlon had a story to tell—something wider and more expansive than the narrow canvas of Sydney cop corruption and white-collar crime—and he felt bound to let her tell it. As if able to read his mind, she reached for the bottle and filled his glass, emptying the dregs into her own.

'I told you and Ms Hardy that I'd had a miscarriage. That wasn't exactly true. I had several. David insisted on the terms of the agreement and he continued to hold off on bringing my mother out. I was able to send her money, but not very much. I couldn't leave him. I have no way to earn a living other than the way I was earning it when I met him. I am vain and lazy. I know that. I was taught to be a lady and then I was taught to be a whore. I could no more work in an office or a factory than fly to the moon.'

She held her manicured, be-ringed hands up, not as emblems of affluence or sexual signals, but as symbols of helplessness.

Dunlop was embarrassed. His original intention, of confronting the woman with some of his conclusions and attempting to induce guilt to coerce information or hints or admissions from her, had evaporated. Here was a different story, going in different directions, and would have a different ending. 'I'm sorry, Mrs Scanlon,' he said quietly. 'I didn't know...'

'Of course not. No-one knew anything. Each time I became pregnant I hoped... and each time I was disappointed. I loved my mother, Mr Dunlop. You cannot imagine what a wonderful woman she was. But I loved David, too. At that time he was, what will I say? Brave and strong will do. Also funny. A good lover, when he was sober. My pregnancies gave me the chance to have absolutely everything I wanted, and each time...'

Dunlop forced himself to divert her back to the area of his concerns. 'Mirabelle,' he said.

'A terrible mistake. After I miscarried for the last time it was made clear that I was unable to have children. David undertook to keep his promise to me about my mother if I agreed to our adopting his illegitimate child. But it... didn't work out. I disliked the child and she disliked me. We fought continuously. David and I fought. And then my mother died. I came to blame him and to hate him and I stayed to make his life a misery. I admit it. It was ignoble of me, but it became my purpose in life. Just as my purpose now is to get drunk. Will you have some more wine?'

Dunlop opened the fridge, took out another bottle and pulled the cork. He poured full glasses, knowing it was a wrong move if Russell was lying in wait for him, but not caring. He was intrigued by the story and believed it. It explained much, but not everything. 'I get the picture,' he said, 'but I don't understand why you threw in with Thomas Kippax against your husband. Unless...'

'I am having an affair with him? Yes, of course I am, but what lies behind that is very strange. Perhaps you won't believe it.' She sipped some wine and coughed, struggled for breath and held up a hand to keep Dunlop back as he leaned towards her. 'I'm all right, thank you. I hadn't picked you for a kind man, Mr Dunlop.'

'You shouldn't,' Dunlop said. 'That'd be a mistake. As for believing you, try me. I believe you so far.'

'I wasn't always barren. Just before I met David I had a child, a girl. I didn't know who the father was until she was born, when it became clear. The girl was very dark, almost black. Do you follow me?'

Dunlop nodded.

'Her father was an American diplomat—very intelligent, very respectable, very black. The child was put out for adoption, of course. A year ago I was given some news of her. She is a whore, as I was, as my mother was. But times are different now, and whores are in grave danger. I can't bear to think of what will happen in Hong Kong when the Chinese take over. I want to bring her to this country, but can you imagine me doing so with David's blessing?'

'It's an amazing story,' Dunlop said.

The rain had stopped and sunshine was breaking through as the clouds cleared. Lucy Scanlon opened the window and allowed some of the cool, fresh air in. 'You are only the second person I have ever told it to,' she said.

'Kippax. Do you think you can trust him?'

She shrugged. 'Oh, I gave up trusting men when I was ten years old. Getting a black whore to Australia is a tricky task. Thomas is powerful and very wealthy. I hope I can use him. I know you think I'm hard, but I have to be. Now, thank you for listening so patiently. You said you wanted to talk to me— what was it about?'

Dunlop finished his wine and stood. He had hoped to drive a wedge between the woman and Kippax, perhaps even to question her about where Scanlon might have secreted his evidence, if he had ever had any to hide. But her story had shown him the futility of that approach.

'It doesn't matter,' he said. 'I suppose I wish you luck with your daughter, but...'

'You had an affinity with David and you liked Mirabelle. I'm sorry, I didn't. It's a very cruel world, Mr Dunlop.'

19

The Ansett flight touched down at Hobart airport a little after noon. Trish Tillotson and Phillip Krabbe had paid cash for their tickets and used false names. They carried only cabin baggage and went quickly through the procedures to take possession of their pre-booked hire car. Phillip used a driver's licence given him by Trish. He wore a grey business suit with blue shirt and red tie. Over his arm he carried a light poplin raincoat because the weather forecast had predicted showers and a temperature considerably lower than Sydney's. Trish had on black slacks, a white silk shirt and a mannish jacket. She wore medium heels and swung her hips slightly as she walked with long strides. As they left the terminal Phillip caught sight of her image in a plate glass window. The look of her thrilled him and the touch of her hand on his arm seemed to fill him with strength.

The red-and-white uniformed Avis woman indicated their car in the parking bay—a blue Ford Camry—and handed Phillip the key. 'Have a nice stay in Tasmania, Mr Jones.'

'Thank you.' Phillip took the key and opened the car. They kissed as soon as they were inside.

'God,' Trish said. 'Planes are sexy. I wanted to haul you off to the toilet for a grope.'

Phillip's hand brushed against her jacket pocket as he took it away from her breast. 'Yes, I know. What's that in your pocket?'

Trish took out the .38 automatic and put it in her shoulder-bag. 'This is business, darling. Remember?'

'But how did you get it through the metal detectors?'

Trish laughed. 'I didn't. I phoned up someone who works at Mascot. She put it in the toilet on the plane for me. You wouldn't believe the amount of stuff that wanders around inside airports. It's simple if you know how.'

Phillip started the car and drove from the open-air parking lot. He was surprised to see how close the hills were. The light had a soft, benign quality and the air was clear and without haze. 'This is nice,' he said.

Trish was consulting the directory she'd taken from the glove box. 'What?'

Phillip negotiated the turn onto a road that ran south. The traffic was amazingly light and moving smoothly. He took his hands from the wheel and gestured exuberantly.

'This.'

'Keep your hands on the wheel,' Trish snapped. 'It'll be as dirty as anywhere else, once you scratch the surface. Especially with Edgar Georges hanging around.'

After the Saab, the Camry was a little sluggish, and Phillip adjusted his driving style to it. 'You haven't told me much about him.'

'There's not much to tell. He was tough and ruthless and fairly smart until the grog and the money got to him. Now he's slow and stupid. Apparently he's scared as well, which is why he's down here. That's our great advantage. Now let's find this Horse Bay. God, it's so small and quiet. I wouldn't live here if you paid me.'

They drove through several coastal townships with Trish navigating. The beach, twenty kilometres from the city centre, stretched away behind a series of dunes. Horse Bay was a tiny cluster of buildings round a small cove and inlet near the southern end of the long, white sand strip.

'Lot 3,' Trish said. 'There it is.'

They pulled up in front of a timber and glass structure with a long, sea-facing deck, a flat roof and high TV mast and solar power unit. It stood in the middle of a half-acre block. A silver-grey Nissan Patrol was parked near the house and the bow of a powerboat poked from a garage. The nearest house was almost a hundred metres away.

'Bought with a bribe,' Trish said.

'Some bribe,' Phillip said. 'What did he do?'

'It's what he *didn't* do. He had the goods on some car importer who was ripping off the government, the exporters, his clients, everyone. No prosecution, and Edgar's got a beach house. I remember the stories about the money at the time. This about fits the amount people guessed at. He probably got the Nissan and the boat the same way.'

Phillip switched off the engine. 'Why here? It sounds as if Queensland would have been more his style.'

Trish climbed from the car, looking around at the landscape with distaste. The area was dominated by

169

Norfolk Island pines and casuarinas, giving it a dark, threatening look. The sky had clouded over and the grass on the dunes was greyish and flattened by the fresh breeze coming off the sea. 'Edgar's a nut. He thinks there's going to be a nuclear war. I remember his talking about his fallout shelter one time when he was pissed, but I guess he thinks he'd really be safest in Tasmania. Also he goes after some kind of fish they've got down here. Don't ask me what it is.'

They tramped up the pebble driveway to the wide wooden steps that led to the deck. There was no garden on the block, just the drive, ivy ground cover and some native shrubs and trees. Trish turned the collar of her jacket up against the breeze and approached the front door. An envelope was thumb-tacked to the wood and she took it down and opened it. Inside was a key, a fifty-dollar note and one of Georges' cards. On the back of the card was written: *Evelyn: Down at the wharf fishing. Please clean up and take away the bottles. Edgar. 1.30 p.m.*

'That's what I hate about the country,' Trish said. 'Everybody knows your fucking business.'

She restored the money and card to the envelope and re-attached it to the door, aware that she was directing the operation too much. She drew a breath and turned to Phillip. 'Should we wait for him here and surprise him? Or go down to the wharf and surprise him? What do you think?'

For his part, Phillip was feeling uncomfortable, out of his element, as he had at the marina in Rush-cutters Bay. He had to assert himself, somehow.

'Let's go to the wharf,' he said. 'If he's as fat as you say he might worry about being pushed in the water.'

170

Trish laughed. 'That'd be a sight to see. Maybe the blubber'd keep him afloat. I like it. The wharf it is.'

A rough track, more suited for four-wheel drives than standard vehicles, led to the wharf. The protection offered by the spits of land that formed the bay was enhanced by a small breakwater, and the stone and timber wharf, more properly a jetty, jutted out into the grey waters just inside it. Several boats were tied up beside the jetty but there was no sign of activity. Phillip took the Camry as far down the track as he dared, but had to stop well short of the cement boat ramp that ran alongside the jetty.

'Not exactly a tourist paradise, is it?' Trish said.

Phillip peered down the length of rough planks and white-painted railing. 'I suppose it's the wrong time of year. The boats all look covered up or battened down, or whatever it's called.'

Trish nodded. 'Can't see him. Has to be behind that shack at the end.'

'Would he have walked to here from the house?'

'Edgar? No way. Must've got a lift. That makes at least two people who know he's here, after Evelyn arrives at the house. Means we can't just dump him in the drink. Pity. Still, he's not to know that.'

They walked along the jetty close together, Phillip sheltering Trish from the light spray coming off the water. Trish pointed to a puff of blue smoke rising from behind the shack. 'Edgar's a serious polluter.'

Phillip nodded. They reached the shack, which occupied half of the end section of the jetty. A gate closed off the other half and Trish gestured for Phillip to open it. They went through and Phillip smelled fish and cigar smoke. Trish sniffed at the combination of odours and put a finger to her lips.

They rounded the shack and saw a rod leaning against the rail, a hessian bag, a bucket, a plastic bag containing bait, other fishing paraphernalia, but no fisherman.

Edgar Georges stepped from a recess behind the shack. He held a short-barrelled pump-action shotgun in his hands and spoke around a cigar stub clamped between his teeth. 'Keep your hands where I can see them, Trish,' he said. 'And the two of you get over here or I'll blow you both apart.'

'Jesus, Edgar,' Trish said. 'What the hell're you playing at?'

'Nobody's playing, Trish. Move.'

'Edgar . . .'

The shotgun moved fractionally and Trish obeyed the movement, stepping sideways, arms and shoulders rigid, eyes fixed on the weapon.

'You knew we were coming,' she said.

'That's right. I just knew about you, actually. Not your friend. But it comes to the same thing. You watch yourself too, sunshine.'

Phillip's legs refused to obey him. He stood, riveted to the spot. His stomach churned and a sourness rose in his throat and threatened to choke him. 'Don't,' he said.

'Move!'

Phillip took two steps, moving jerkily like a badly manipulated marionette. He found himself beside Trish at the top of a set of steps that led down to the water. His head jerked up when he heard the engine of a powerboat churning the water. A sleek red cruiser slid through the choppy waves towards the jetty.

'Down!'

172

Trish stood on the first step and looked up at Phillip. 'I'm sorry, lover,' she said.

The boat drew closer. There were two men in it. One held a pistol casually, pointing it vaguely in the direction of the jetty.

'What... what d... do you mean?'

'Get your shoes wet, Trish,' Georges said.

Trish went down two steps. The water splashed up around her feet.

Georges spat out his cigar stub. 'You too, lover.'

Phillip stumbled down the steps. Trish gripped his arm and they waited, lapped by the waterline. The cruiser engine died and it drifted in towards the jetty. The man with the pistol levelled it at Trish and Phillip, untroubled by the rise and fall, while the driver jockeyed the boat close to the steps. It bumped. The boatman threw a rope around a pylon.

'Pretty dumb moves for you, Trish,' Georges said. 'I never knew you to be cock-struck before. Take the gun out of your pocket and drop it into the water. Slowly. I've got a clear shot at you and lover boy, but it might not be too clean.'

Trish's hand moved to her pocket. Slowly, she lifted the automatic free and let it fall. It bounced on a submerged step and Trish watched it slip sideways and disappear. 'Any chance of a deal, Edgar? For old times' sake?'

'No chance. Sorry, Trish. You lose this one. You had a good run. Get in the boat.'

Phillip was sobbing and would have fallen if Trish hadn't supported him. They stepped into the boat. Phillip looked up through eyes blurred by tears at the fat man with the shotgun 'Listen, Mr Georges, I'm Phillip Krabbe. My father...'

'A good mate of mine. You should have listened to him. Sorry, son. Okay, take it away.'

Trish said, 'He'll get you too, Edgar. Call this off now and we can squeeze him dry.'

Georges shook his head. 'He's too big and I've got all I need.'

The boatman unlooped the line, pushed off from the jetty and started the engine. He transferred his weapon to his left hand, held it steady, picked up a length of pipe wrapped in insulating tape and used it to prod first Phillip, then Trish in the small of the back.

'Lie down!'

At the touch of the pipe, Trish slipped her shoulder-bag down, grasped the strap, crouched, turned and swung. Although she was quick, she was off-balance and the gunman seemed to have seconds to spare. He avoided the swinging bag, swept the pipe up and crashed it against her temple. She collapsed. The bag skidded across the boat's engine canopy and fell into the sea.

'Said she had guts,' the gunman grunted. 'Lie down, you!'

Phillip's knees buckled and he lay weeping beside Trish in the bottom of the boat. The gunman swung the pipe in a short arc and shattered his skull. He changed his grip and swung again, bringing the pipe down on Trish's head with colossal force. Bone fragments, blood and brain matter spattered the boatman, who swore.

Edgar Georges waddled across the jetty and slid the shotgun into the hessian sack. He bent with an effort and took a small crab from his plastic bag. Then he baited his hook, checked the tackle and cast expertly out into the grey-green water.

20

Dunlop became aware of the car following him after his dawn visit to Trish Tillotson's flat. He'd gone there the day after his call on Lucy Scanlon and waited through the evening until midnight. Then he went home and tried to sleep. He managed a restless two hours of dozing before coming back as light appeared in the sky. He'd opened the security door and rung the bell at Flat 4.

Nothing. He knew she wasn't at the trainees' hostel where she was, nominally, a warden. He knew she hadn't been at her desk for the past twenty-four hours. The team studying criminal profiling seemed to be getting along fine without her. It seemed to Dunlop that everybody was getting along fine without Dave and Mirabelle Scanlon too, except him. He and Tillotson and her tall, fair friend were the only people who knew the girl was dead. It mattered to him. He couldn't let it rest.

He was frustrated and he knew he was disoriented from lack of sleep. Good sense said take Burton's offer. Retire on medical grounds with a pension. Go to Queensland. Work on his putting. Get a single-figure handicap. Find a nice woman who'd never twisted an arm, never pulled a body from a car wreck, never fired a gun. A woman who'd go fishing with him and read Le Carré novels and grow vegetables. He couldn't do it. At least, not yet. He watched the blue Commodore in his rear-vision mirror as it did a fair job of avoiding being spotted. The driver hung back, changed lanes, made the turns late. But if you knew how to do it, you knew how to spot it. That was one of the problems. Dunlop felt the adrenalin pumping into his already over-charged, under-nourished system. He liked the feeling. *Follow me, would you, you fucker? I'll show you a thing or two.*

He drove towards Marrickville, taking no evasive action, using the obvious route. The street he turned into off Stanmore Road ended abruptly at a fence that enclosed part of a school ground. The No Through Road sign was obscured by the branches of a plane tree that the council workers habitually failed to prune. The short street—occupied for most of its length by a factory on one side and a nursing home on the other, rose sharply and looked as if it would continue through beyond the hill. Dunlop went over the rise and whipped the Laser into a sharp turn. He mounted the nature strip with his off-side wheels and was around, heading back, when the Commodore came cautiously forward. Dunlop gunned the motor, spun the wheel and pulled up behind the Commodore, which braked sharply and stalled when it met the cul-de-sac gutter.

Dunlop leapt out, ran forward and had his pistol at the temple of the driver before he could touch the gearshift. The man in the passenger seat raised his hands.

176

'Good,' Dunlop said. 'That's very good. Hands nicely up without even asking. Why're you two clowns following me?'

Neither man spoke. The driver's hands stayed on the wheel. The other man turned his head slowly and looked at Dunlop. He saw a wild-eyed pistol-holder with two days' growth, wearing a shirt that looked like a rag. The street was quiet and still. It was barely light. The asphalt-coated schoolyard was misty and the rubbish tins looked like gravestones. He tried to speak but his throat and mouth had dried and no sound emerged.

Dunlop jabbed the pistol into the driver's ear. The man screeched and Dunlop dug the metal in again. 'You heard the question. I can do you both and drive away. I'm in the mood for it. Tell me!'

The driver gulped and found speech. 'Hell, man. A job. Nothing personal.'

Dunlop was on the edge and the American accent threatened to tip him over. Dave Scanlon was dead, Mirabelle was dead. Why not these two? 'You've got two seconds to tell me who you're working for. Or you can die. The way I'm feeling it makes no bloody difference to me either way.'

'Okay, okay, man. I believe you. But we don't know. Honest.'

Dunlop touched the pistol to the battered ear. 'Not good enough, Yank. So long.'

'Wait on, wait on. We got a number to call. That's all we got. I swear it.'

'Tell me the number. Speak clearly. Come on, don't think, say it!'

The driver's hands shook as he gripped the steering wheel. 'I ... we ...'

'Come on!'

The other man stared at Dunlop and lowered his hands. 'The fucking phone's on redial. That's it. We were just supposed to call in. See where you went, who you met. Shit like that. Nothing heavy.'

Dunlop looked into the back of the car and saw two cameras and surveillance equipment. His racing pulse slowed a few beats and he took the trouble to examine the men. Neither looked like an enforcer and yet, just for a couple of minutes, he'd seen them as assassins. 'I get it,' he said. 'You need to brush up on your technique. Okay, release the phone and hand it to me slowly. When I've got it, you're free to go.'

The driver brushed away blood from his neck and took the mobile phone from its cradle. He passed it through the window. Dunlop gripped the sticky plastic surface and stepped back from the car.

'Piss off.'

The driver shoved the Commodore into reverse, revved and let the big car plough back into the front of the Laser. Even at that short distance, the impact was considerable, crumpling the Laser's front bumper, radiator and left headlight. Dunlop swore but had to move away quickly as the driver wrenched the wheel and accelerated, hitting Dunlop's car a glancing blow and narrowly missing Dunlop himself as it roared back up the street. Dogs barked and there was movement in the front of the nursing home. Dunlop swore as he inspected the car. It looked to be driveable. He put his pistol in the glove box and laid the mobile phone on the passenger seat. The engine fired and there was only a slight pinging of metal and rubber brushing together as he U-turned and drove away.

178

Tiredness hit him as he defused the garage alarm and walked through the overgrown backyard into his house. For a time he had maintained the grass and shrubs in the yard and made serious attempts at growing vegetables. But increasing case loads and growing disenchantment with the work had caused him to neglect the property. The grass was knee high in places; the vegetable bed was a tangle of thistle and weeds. Neighbourhood cats took advantage of the fact that he had no pets of his own to use the backyard as a place to piss and shit. A broken window and several roof tiles, displaced in a winter storm, still awaited repair. The sight of the run-down place depressed him. The large garbage bin was overflowing and the stacks of yellowed news-paper—supposed to be put out for recycling but regularly forgotten—were escaping from their string bindings.

'You're becoming a slob,' he said. 'And you're talking to yourself like a loony.'

He made instant coffee and grimaced when the milk he added left flecks on the surface. He spooned in sugar and undertook to drink it anyway. He took the mobile phone through to his workroom, sipped some of the half-sour, half-sweet coffee and pressed the redial button. The number came up big and clear on the phone's digital display. He copied it down and hung up.

'Got you, you bastard.'

It was six-thirty a.m. and he was suddenly tired to the bone, but he had a purpose. He finished the coffee, showered, washed his hair, shaved and changed into clean clothes. He cleaned his teeth and flossed them, scraped the dirt from his fingernails.

He went to the shop at the corner of Addison Road and bought ground coffee, milk, two croissants and the morning paper, exchanging smiles and nods with the Vietnamese and Greek and Turkish neighbours who were starting their reluctant cars, watering their front gardens, seeing their neatly attired children off to school. The normalcy of it all gave him energy and enthusiasm. The morning had dawned bright and clear. High clouds had gathered in the west but would probably pass over. He poured the sour milk down the sink and ran the tap on it. He heated his croissants without burning them, buttered them and made coffee that gave off an aroma that seemed to clear his head. He forced himself to eat and drink slowly, to taste the food and drink, to keep his brain in neutral. He rinsed the plate and knife, poured another cup of coffee and took it into the workroom.

Dunlop's computer was still hooked up to the Federal police, New South Wales police, WPU and SCCA data banks. He could access a wide span of other material as well—government employees, permanent and contractual, company registers, credit card records, motor vehicle and licence entries, medical files and telephone information, including number and subscriber cross listings. He switched on the computer, logged up the relevant software, and entered the number he'd taken from the mobile phone. The computer confirmed that it was a valid entry and Dunlop's request for information on the subscriber resulted in the words KRABBE CONSULTANCY LTD appearing on the screen.

'Krabbe,' Dunlop said. 'Jesus Christ, how many more cops do I have to run into on this bloody thing?'

He accessed the company files and entered the name. Krabbe Consultancy was listed as a private company with an address in Woolloomooloo. The managing director was Phillip Arnold Krabbe, LLB, MBA, aged thirty, single, address in Rose Bay; father Keith Krabbe, police officer, mother Sylvia, nee Anderson. He worked for an hour, pursuing Krabbe through a variety of channels, picking up snippets of information and collecting them in a single file. When he'd finished he had a comprehensive word portrait of the young executive. Among other vehicles, Krabbe Consultancy leased a royal blue Saab sedan. Dunlop saved what he thought of as the best for last, entering a request for a facsimile copy of Krabbe's driver's licence. He made more coffee and was holding a mug of the fresh brew diluted by the fresh milk when the fax came through. Even making allowances for the poor quality of the photograph and the distortions of facsimile transmission, there could be no doubt: Phillip Arnold Krabbe was the man he had seen with Detective Sergeant Patricia Tillotson leaving the garage in Bellevue Hill that had contained the body of Mirabelle Scanlon.

Dunlop sipped the milky coffee and considered whether it was worthwhile approaching Burton and the police with this discovery. He decided against doing so. Krabbe was a lawyer, no doubt safe-guarded by all the defences lawyers had built into the system to protect themselves. Nevertheless, he assembled the material into a coherent file and printed out a hard copy. Weariness that the coffee had only just held at bay was threatening to over-whelm him. He produced three more dossiers before he abandoned the computer—on Thomas

Kippax, Trish Tillotson and Keith Krabbe. None contained anything immediately significant but the routine act of assembling them was oddly satisfying. He felt the settling down of his jangled nerves. His mental pictures of Dave and Mirabelle, sharp-edged by death, began to blur. As he tapped the keys he saw that the knuckles he'd scraped at some time in the last few days—when boarding the *Mirabelle*, getting Scanlon to hospital, or in subduing Geoff and Russell—had begun to heal. He took off his clothes as the files printed out and stumbled towards his unmade bed.

'So, now you can marry me, Thomas,' Lucy Scanlon said. 'And we can live happily ever after.'

Kippax's waxy skin paled still further as he sipped his drink. They were sitting on the balcony of his apartment in the Connaught. He had not wanted the meeting, not so soon after Scanlon's death and the flurry of activity that had followed it, but Lucy had insisted. Now she laughed at his evident distress.

'Only joking, darling. I know you're married to your work. And things will proceed . . . more smoothly now, I trust.'

Kippax struggled not to show his relief. 'I trust so. But I still feel that this meeting was indiscreet.'

Lucy rearranged the folds of her dark dress. Proud of her legs and aware of her lack of height, she had avoided the currently fashionable low-topped, long-skirted look for some time but was pleased with her first venture into the new style. Reasonably widow-like, she thought, but she'd also noticed Kippax's surreptitious attempts to see more

182

than the skirt revealed. 'I'm in a mood for indiscretion. You're a cold fish, Thomas Kippax, but I admire you. You know what you want and you go after it. I'm much the same.'

Kippax thought he could see where the conversation was tending. He found her intensely attractive and especially appreciated the stimulating effects of some of the practices she had introduced him to. Since receiving a cryptic, but clear to him, message from Edgar Georges, he had felt safer. He hoped that Lucy was not going to pose a new threat in her turn. He'd had enough of threats. It was time to draw back from the cut-and-thrust, consolidate, and even indulge himself. The SCCA inquiry would fizzle to nothing without Scanlon. He was safe on that front.

Kippax stared out over the dark green expanse of Hyde Park. His view of the harbour was slightly impeded by several buildings, something he hadn't appreciated when he bought the apartment. He needed to be several floors higher. It was irritating. His intention had only ever been to secure a dominance in a lucrative market. An unassailable position, and he had never been quite able to grasp why he'd met with resistance and had had to resort to unorthodox tactics to secure his ends. As he became older he'd found that thoughts of this kind had increasingly come to distract him from the business at hand. It required an effort to shake them off.

'You're talking about the woman in Hong Kong, I assume?' he barked.

'My daughter, yes.'

Kippax had several children, daughters included, from an early, unwise marriage. He had not seen them for a great many years and was unsure of their names, following the changes flowing from his ex-wife's remarriages. He seldom thought about them and considered that the trust fund arrangements he had made discharged his responsibility. Lucy's concern for this by-blow puzzled him. He finished his drink, a strong one for him, and felt the juices flow. He wanted to see her naked and watch her urinate and defecate. The sight of her functions excited him and produced intense if short-lived erections. Lucy was an expert in putting that momentary blood rush to good use. He wanted it all to happen now.

'I'll have her here as soon as it's humanly possible,' he said throatily.

Got him, Lucy thought triumphantly. *But he's still too smug and sure of himself. I need more than just this to hold him.* She unbuttoned her dress and slipped out of it to stand in front of him in her brassiere and panties, gartered stockings and high-heeled shoes. She allowed a little urine to flow, took off the damp panties and handed them to him.

Kippax allowed the wet silkiness to slide around in his hands, transported by the touch and smell. He followed her towards the bathroom, watching the undulations of her tight buttocks. The bathroom was a huge, pink-tiled expanse with a vast mirror behind a lavishly appointed vanity unit, heated towel racks, modular shower recess, sauna and a nine-metre-square spa bath. Lucy removed her shoes and brassiere and stepped into the spa bath. She spread her legs and beckoned Kippax forward.

He moved like a man in a dream, dropping the wet pants and extending his hands. Lucy placed his pale hands under her crotch, sighed and raised her hands to her small, firm breasts. *This part of it's all right,* she thought. *Almost fun. If I can make it good enough, maybe he'll come and I won't have to shit in his hair.* She relaxed the muscles and allowed the urine to flow over his cupped hands. He moaned and leaned against the edge of the spa bath, his erection straining inside his trousers. He unzipped himself, wetting his clothes and releasing his thin, mottled penis.

But I need that extra grip, Lucy thought. She turned around and spread her buttocks, hearing keys and coins jingle in his pockets as he sank to the floor and craned forward. *When his hair's full of it and he's spurting, I'll ask him about Dunlop.*

21

Dunlop woke at ten a.m. feeling human for the first time in days. He went naked to the bathroom, rinsed his face in cold water and combed his hair. Less skinfold but more lines, more grey, more plaque. He refused to let it bother him. He wrapped a towel around his waist, made scrambled eggs and toast and ate them with some re-heated coffee. He cleaned his teeth. Two teeth-cleanings and two breakfasts in one day—a record. Two more than some days. Maybe he could become fat, happy Lucas Dunlop yet. He set the mobile phone on the kitchen table and pressed the redial button.

'Yes?'

'Krabbe Consultants?'

No response.

Dunlop drew in a breath. 'Mr Phillip Krabbe, please.'

The phone went dead. Dunlop called again. The number rang for half a minute, then the call was accepted and immediately cut off.

'Trouble at the ranch,' Dunlop said. He looked out the dusty window at the emerging day. The sky was overcast, but the cloud was high and there were breaks to the east. A light breeze was stirring the modest Marrickville street trees. He put on a light-weight grey suit, pale blue shirt and burgundy tie. His black shoes were scuffed and he applied liquid polish restoratively. The file on Phillip Krabbe he packed into a briefcase along with the mobile phone. The recently lost weight left him plenty of room inside the suit jacket for a shoulder harness and his .38 pistol. He dumped the dishes in the sink, collected cards, keys and money and went out to the garage. He didn't notice the weeds or smell the cat piss.

Dunlop walked across the paved courtyard, follow-ing the sign pointing to Krabbe Consultancy's suite of offices. His feet crunched on fallen leaves and he could smell the chlorine in the complex's swimming pool. Nice work if you could get it. Everything made of wood was oiled and weather-proofed; the glass was tinted and non-reflecting; the metal surfaces were polished. A male and two female smokers indulged their habit furtively in a corner of the courtyard. They looked up defensively as he went past. To the best of Dunlop's knowledge, lung cancer rates had increased since filters were introduced and packets of thirty had counteracted the possible benefits of lower tar and nicotine content. He was tolerant of smokers, as long as they didn't do it near him, and admired their defiance, as long as they didn't whinge when the whip came down.

He entered the door marked KRABBE CONSULT-ANCY SERVICES, swinging his briefcase. The young woman at the reception desk looked at him as if he were carrying a baseball bat, cocked, ready to swing.

'Yes, yes, sir?'

'I want to see Mr Phillip Krabbe.' Dunlop took his wallet from his breast pocket, perhaps showing the pistol, hard to be sure, and removed a card. It identified him as an officer of the Federal police force. 'Please tell him I'm here.'

'I can't. I mean, I'm afraid you can't see him.'

'Why not? No appointment? This is an important matter. Police business. I insist on seeing him.'

'It's ... not possible, at this time.'

'All right. I'd like to see his ... what would it be, manager? The second in charge?'

'There is no such person.'

Dunlop spun around slowly, taking in the thick carpet, pot-plants, the opulent reception desk, open-plan work space behind it with several private offices that appeared to overlook the bay. Only one of the three desks was occupied and the woman sitting at it appeared to be struggling to find anything to do. The office doors were closed and the whole place was alarmingly quiet. A photocopying machine beside the reception desk had not been turned on; all the filing cabinets were closed; even the pot-plants appeared somewhat wilted.

'I don't understand,' Dunlop said. 'Is this a place of business or not?'

The receptionist was clearly too distressed to answer. Dunlop was sympathetic but felt he had to press home the advantage. 'Very well,' he said. 'Could I make an appointment with Mr Krabbe for, say, Friday? At ten-thirty?'

The receptionist flipped open a book. Dunlop saw three days' worth of appointments unfulfilled and uncancelled. The receptionist turned the pages eagerly, clumsily. 'Yes. Yes, that will be fine, Mr...' she squinted at the card, 'Dunlap.'

'Dunlop.'

She wrote in the book, relieved to have something concrete to do. 'Mr Lucas Dunlop. Yes.'

'Thank you.'

Dunlop left the office. *What was the name of that ship with no captain and no crew?* he thought. *The Marie Celeste.* The receptionist would have made him an appointment for any time from an hour ahead to the end of the century, just to get rid of him. She had no idea of where her boss was or when he'd next turn up.

Dunlop spent the new few hours confirming his impression that Detective Sergeant Patricia Tillotson had not been sighted at work or at her usual haunts for the past three days. He drove to Rose Bay and found Krabbe's Saab parked neatly in its allotted undercover space. His skill with the pick-locks got him into the building, an old red brick block of flats, extensively modernised, and past the substantial security system installed at Krabbe's apartment. Dunlop felt almost as if he were on a training exercise—obstacles thrown up, tricky, but possible to overcome so as not to discourage the learners.

He was on edge again, the result of asking questions, lying and being lied to, opening locked doors. It was late in the afternoon and the food and drink of the morning were a memory. He prowled around in the big flat, noting the expensive hi-fi equipment and VCR and the small stock of CDs and videotapes. The books were mostly on economics and business management theory. A set of Cobra golf clubs looked as if they had never been used, likewise two Emrik tennis rackets. The Nike joggers had been for a few runs though and a football had been frequently handled. *Jogging and touch football,* Dunlop thought. *Fit, but fit for what?*

The bed had been hastily made up after two people had slept in it. There were two condoms wrapped in face tissues in the bathroom waste bin. The hairbrush held a number of fair hairs and a couple of dark ones, thicker and slightly kinked. Dunlop opened the fridge, took out a stubby of Cooper's light beer and ripped the cap off. He leaned against the sink, drank, and sorted impressions: Krabbe and Tillotson were a team; they'd taken off for parts unknown—not overseas, because Krabbe's passport was still in a desk drawer. Very little disturbance of the clothes, shoes, luggage etc. Travelling light. But travelling where and why? Not running, but not advertising the departure—otherwise, why not take the Saab?

Dunlop finished the beer, placed the bottle and the cap near the door, and did another search of the flat. He worked patiently through the Rolodex but learned little other than that Krabbe had hundreds of business numbers listed—including several for Thomas Kippax, but the same for other prominent media figures—and a scant five or six for what could be friends and acquaintances. Touch footballers, most likely. No women. *You were a sitting duck for our Trish, mate,* Dunlop thought. The telephone rang several times, but Dunlop ignored it, assuming the office was trying to make contact with the boss. He had no suggestions to offer. He took a note of the three numbers for Keith Krabbe and abandoned the Rolodex.

Krabbe's chequebooks were in a drawer; a dry-cleaning slip indicated that he'd had a suit ready for collection a day before. The man had intended to be gone for a day or two at the most. Dunlop found a small key by the telephone, took a chance on objecting neighbours, and unlocked Krabbe's mailbox. Several days' worth of letters had collected. Therefore, no redirection of mail, no intention of a long absence. Back in the flat he cast around desperately for some clue. An empty hanger in a closet, between a tweed overcoat and dark, formal topcoat, suggested that Krabbe had taken a coat of some kind. Dunlop's anger and frustration tempted him to break something in the affluent, fussily organised surroundings. He resisted the impulse, collected up the evidence of his intrusion and left the flat.

'Fears are held for the life of Sydney Detective Sergeant Patricia Tillotson, who has been absent from work and her home for the past three days. A bag containing Detective Tillotson's credit cards and other documents was found washed up on a Tasmanian beach earlier today. Police say they are puzzled by the discovery. Detective Tillotson was not on leave and her current duties as a member of a special unit investigating modern criminal profiling techniques did not require her to travel to Tasmania. Detective Tillotson, who has figured in many arrests of violent criminals, has a reputation as one of the toughest female officers in the New South Wales force. Investigation is continuing…'

Thomas Kippax switched off the television set and leaned back in his chair. Sweat broke out on his forehead and he could feel the blood pumping and the pressure building up behind his eyes. A migraine on the way. It had been a stressful day at the office with more than the usual number of difficult decisions to make himself and several others to unmake. Lucy Scanlon's attentions the night before had left him oddly depleted. In the past, the sexual release had fired him up for business activity. Finding a woman of reasonable refinement who understood his needs had been a boon, but on this occasion she had pressed him hard on the difficult and distasteful subject of her mongrel daughter. Added to that had been the implied threat. Dunlop. A formidable figure, evidently. Kippax had begun to think in terms of a massive bribe. And now this!

He made himself a scotch and water. *Another bad sign*, he thought. *Drinking alone*. Something he scrupulously avoided. But he knew he would need the drink when the phone rang—which it did, within minutes.

'Yes.'

'You've heard the news,' Edgar Georges said.

'Of course. I can hardly believe you could be so incompetent.'

'One of those things. You can't cover everything. It must've happened after... my involvement. Everything was okay at that point, I can assure you.'

'Assure me! What a moronic thing to say. How can you assure me of anything? This could lead in all sorts of directions. She was...'

'Watch what you say. There's more and you're not going to like it.'

192

Kippax sipped his drink, wishing he'd made it stronger. The headache was building and the whisky would make it worse. He looked around the apartment—three Whiteleys on the wall, from a good period, sure to appreciate now that the artist was dead. One hundred thousand dollars' worth of carpet. It all seemed suddenly insubstantial and meaningless. 'Tell me.'

'There was a companion. You know who. He went on the same trip.'

'Jesus.'

'It couldn't be done any other way.'

'Christ.'

'I'm taking a trip myself. Business. I'd advise you to do the same until it blows over. Which it will. Don't worry.'

Kippax's mind seethed. He wanted to ask about the bodies and the chances of their being found. He wanted to talk about Dunlop. He wanted to explain that he couldn't drop everything and leave the country. He had to satisfy Lucy Scanlon and quickly. He had an empire to administer and no-one trustworthy to delegate to. The phone went dead in his hand and he slowly replaced it and became aware again of the glass in his hand. He finished the drink and went in search of his migraine medicine. The pain was mounting, blotting out the problems, blotting out everything.

22

Two days later, Dunlop sat in Keith Krabbe's office on the third floor of the police building in College Street. Krabbe held the rank of Chief Inspector. Many, inside and outside the force, considered it a miracle that he was still a policeman at all, let alone the holder of a senior rank. An enforcer for the most corrupt elements in politics, policing and business in the Askin era and subsequently, Krabbe had been singled out for criticism in several Royal Commissions and other inquiries, suspended, investigated and written about by journalists. Anecdotally, he was a principal in five murders and involved in several more. The reason for his survival was simple—Keith Krabbe had more dirt on others than they had on him. He was sidelined, bypassed, put out to graze to wait for his pension, but still intensely feared. He had aspired to the Commissionership and was a bitterly disappointed man.

Dunlop had refused coffee and cigarettes. Krabbe, a medium-sized man with a compact figure and a full head of dark blond hair despite his age, sat behind his desk and unwrapped a stick of chewing gum. 'I'm not going to pretend I'm busy,' he said.

'But you can get on with whatever you've got to say as soon as you like.'

Dunlop unzipped his briefcase. 'It's about your son, Phillip. When did you last hear from him?'

'I said get on with it.'

Dunlop laid papers on the desk. 'This is the way I see it, Keith. Somehow your boy got into harness with Trish Tillotson doing a job for Thomas Kippax.'

Krabbe chewed vigorously and said nothing.

'I saw them together. They'd taken Dave Scanlon's daughter off his boat and put her in Trish's garage. She was dead. I don't know how or why.'

'Proof?'

'No. This isn't about proof. This is about what happened. You should know the difference. You did things, I've done things, but no-one could ever prove it. You know what I mean.'

Krabbe had heard about how Dunlop had been railroaded out of the police force. He'd also heard about Dunlop and Kerry Loew. 'I'm listening.'

'I think Trish and Phillip went down to Tasmania to see Edgar Georges. He's got a place down there. Near where Trish's bag washed up. I don't know why. Maybe working for Kippax still, maybe working against him. They didn't come back. Edgar's taken off for Vanuatu or some such fucking place and Kippax's lying low. You'll never see your son again, Keith. Your old mate Edgar's fed him to the fishes.'

'Fuck you!' Krabbe said. 'This is all hot air.'

Dunlop shook his head. 'I saw them together. I saw his car in Trish's garage. She spent the night in his flat before they disappeared. They weren't planning to be gone long, but...'

Krabbe's rugged face was bleak, his pale eyes behind the rimless spectacles expressionless. 'Can you show me anything to back this up?'

'Not much.' Dunlop took the mobile phone from his bag. 'This was being carried by a couple of characters who were following me. I relieved them of it. It was keyed in to Phillip's office. I've got phone records of calls between Phillip and Kippax...'

'Nothing in that,' Krabbe grunted.

'Look, Dave Scanlon had the goods on Kippax and was going to spill. Kippax used Trish, Edgar Georges and Phillip to put the pressure on Dave. That worked.'

'You mean you fucked up. I read the papers.'

'You do more than read the papers, you *know* what's going on. Dave's dead, his daughter's dead, Trish's dead, Phillip hasn't been sighted by anyone for a week. Edgar's out of reach. I've resigned from the WPU, or you could say I've had the boot. Doesn't make much difference. Who's still standing?'

Krabbe got up and began to pace behind his desk. He scowled out of the window at the city skyline and chewed hard on his gum. 'Suppose you're right, what the fuck do you want me to do about it? I can barely get an order for a packet of paper clips through these days.'

'How's your wife handling it?'

'You cunt!'

'Let's stop pissing around, Keith. You know I'm right. You can smell it. As far as I'm concerned, Kippax killed Dave and the girl and got me in the shit. Trish and your boy are out of it. I want Kippax and I don't much care how I get him.'

Krabbe shook his head. 'I don't believe this. You're not talking about...'

'No. You're too old for that line of work any more.'

'It feels like I'm too old for everything. How could Phil have got involved with that bitch? I don't understand it. But then, I never understood the boy at all, not from the time he was little. We didn't agree about a single thing, and now...'

Dunlop waited, embarrassed, while Krabbe wiped his eyes and blew his nose. He took off his glasses and massaged the indentation they had made on the bridge of his beaked nose. 'Edgar,' he said.

'Not Edgar. He's the messenger boy. Kippax.'

Krabbe shook his head and replaced his glasses. 'Too big.'

Dunlop leaned forward as if to exert physical pressure on the shaken man across the desk. He spoke quietly, telling Krabbe what Scanlon had revealed about his involvement in the death of Kippax's brother. Krabbe held up his hand.

'Before you go on, stand up, take off your shirt and drop your trousers.'

Dunlop did as instructed. 'No wires, Keith. This is just between you and me.'

'Okay. Just between you and me, Dave was probably telling the truth. I heard about it. They fixed the bloke's car. I remember the funeral. Big turnout. But it won't do you any good. The man who did the job's dying of cancer.'

'McCausland?'

Krabbe nodded. 'He may be on the way out, but he's got a hell of a lot to protect. You wouldn't get a squeak from him.'

'He wouldn't do a thing for me anyway, and I wouldn't ask him. He set me up for the trouble that got me off the force. But that's not it. Dave said he had a videotape that proved Kippax was in on the murder of the brother.'

Krabbe removed his glasses again and jiggled them, stressing the arms. 'Could be. Dave was into all that sort of shit pretty early. He videoed his fucking boats, his golf swing, all that.'

'You knew him pretty well in the old days. If he had something like that, something that important— where would he hide it?'

'Safety deposit box?'

Dunlop shook his head.

'You check his boat?'

'Tore it apart. Nothing.'

'Which one?'

'How do you mean?'

'There's an old boat, the first one he had. Couldn't bear to sell it. Last I heard it was in a slipway at Balmain. He paid money just to keep it there, high and dry. Fucking crazy, these boat nuts.'

'What's its name?'

Krabbe looked tired and old. 'Jesus, I dunno. I'm going to have to tell my wife about Phillip. What am I going to say? Why couldn't he have... Shit, don't look at me like that, I tell you I don't know. What's his wife's name?'

'Lucille. Lucy.'

Krabbe shook his head. 'No, that's not it. Mirabelle. Yeah, his kid's name. Mirabelle.'

The slipway was at the bottom of Duke Street in East Balmain. The boatyard had seen better days and was in danger of being extinguished by a combination of foreshore reclamation and town house development. Dunlop used his by now highly questionable Federal police credentials to get the attention of the senior of the two boat builders at work among the vessels. He was shown a small, weather-beaten sailing boat, sitting on supports in a corner of the yard.

'Belongs to a cop,' the boat builder told him. 'Was a nice boat once. Mate of yours?'

'Sort of,' Dunlop said. 'He died a few days ago. This isn't a police matter. I'm thinking of buying it.'

'Needs a lot of work. Be glad to help. Well, take a look and see what you think.'

'Can you lend me an overall? I might want to crawl around a bit.'

Dunlop's ex-wife, Katarina (or, rather, Frank Carter's ex-wife), had been an enthusiastic sailor. Dunlop had tried to share her enthusiasm and had crewed for her in several harbour races, but he found the sport unsatisfying. The periods of inactivity followed by frantic, hectic outpourings of energy did not suit his temperament. Nevertheless, he had picked up enough knowledge about boats to understand their construction and the function of the different sections and compartments. The sail locker, the most obvious hiding place, held a tool chest but, as he expected, nothing else. Likewise the recess where the life jackets were stored and the space around the first aid chest.

He crawled around, tapping, probing and measuring, trying to find hollownesses, discrepancies between internal and exterior dimensions, blank spaces, anything out of place in the tight, economical construction of a small sailing boat. He found nothing and sat in the stern with his hand resting idly on the tiller. He remembered Katarina's instructions—'reef', 'furl', 'tack', but no longer recalled exactly what the terms meant. It was a long time ago, all packed up and deposited on a memory shelf. Dusty. Almost forgotten and better so. He stared down the length of the boat, letting his eye run along the mast which lay, unstepped, out of the well where it would lock in and be held firm when it carried sails and invited the wind.

Moving like an automaton, Dunlop went forward, bent and put his hand into the slot where the mast would sit. He felt an obstruction, a metal barrier. He scrabbled around its edges and found it a tight fit. He took the tool kit out and used a thin-bladed screwdriver to prise up an aluminium oblong. He lifted it free. He let his fingers feel around in the space below and they encountered a smooth, greasy surface, then a different texture—plastic wrapping and insulation tape. His heart was thudding and he was sweating freely inside the hot overall. He wiped his face with the back of his hand and pulled up the package. Allowing for the taping and heavy wrapping, it measured approximately 190 by 100 centimetres—the right size for a VHS video cassette. Dunlop kissed it and then spat away the taste of the grease that had been applied thickly over the whole surface.

'Good on you, Dave,' he said.

23

'**M**y name is David Rodney Scanlon and I was formerly an officer in the New South Wales police force with the rank of Detective Inspector. In January 1983, I conspired with Walter Loomis and Ian McCausland, also police officers, and Thomas Kippax, a magazine publisher, to murder Louis Kippax, who was then the co-head, with Thomas, of Kippax Publishing.

'McCausland, who is an expert mechanic, tampered with the brakes of Terence Kippax's Daimler so that they would fail when a certain pressure was applied on a certain gradient. Loomis spent time with Louis Kippax on the night of his death, ensuring that he became drunk and persuading him to drive home by a particular route, one of two Kippax normally took.

'My role was to make sure that no inconvenient inquiries were made into what was judged to be an accident and to coordinate Thomas Kippax's payments to McCausland, Loomis and myself. For these services, McCausland received fifty thousand dollars and Loomis and myself thirty thousand.

'What follows is a videotape record of McCausland

201

explaining to Kippax how the accident was to be arranged. The sound quality is poor owing to the necessity of muffling the camera's electric motor.'

Dunlop stared, fascinated, at the screen as the clearly focused and lit image of Scanlon sitting quietly in shirtsleeves in what looked like the den of his house, was replaced by a grainy picture of two men standing in a garage. A vehicle was parked by the opening and the camera zoomed in briefly on its licence plate. The car was a Jaguar, presumably Kippax's. Dunlop recognised McCausland, a short, wide man with a snub nose and aggressive manner. He had only ever seen photographs of Kippax, and had one by him now at the head of a letter from the publisher in a copy of *Business Daily*. The tallish, austere-looking person, whose skin had an unhealthy pallor, fitted the bill. McCausland held up two pieces of cable and a length of tube. His Belfast boyhood was still in his speech patterns:

> *McCAUSLAND: You cut through this here, just so far, and you make a hole just below the brake fluid cylinder. It's fuckin' delicate work to do it properly. That's why it's worth fifty.*
> *KIPPAX: I see.*
> *McCAUSLAND: He comes down that hill, heavy car, and he's a bit pissed if Walter's been on the job properly—goin' too fuckin' fast, most likely. He pumps hard to get braking, doesn't get enough and pumps harder. The cable gives and he's history on that road.*
> *KIPPAX: And you can do this tonight?*
> *McCAUSLAND: It's fuckin' done, and I've given you a bonus.*

KIPPAX: *I don't… understand.*

McCAUSLAND: *Don't worry about it. I can't fuckin' see why you wanted to know this much, but that's all you need to know.*

KIPPAX: *Very well. Thank you.*

McCAUSLAND: *I'll thank Dave and he'll thank you. Okay?*

The screen went blank and then Scanlon appeared again.

'McCausland had made sure that the petrol tank would leak and cause a fire when the car rolled or when it came to a stop. That's what more or less happened and the evidence of the tampering with the brakes was destroyed. One of the insurance investigators who inspected the vehicle raised some technical questions about the accident and prepared a report. I was informed of this and exerted pressure on this man to change the document. Copies of the original and revised report are enclosed in this package along with banking records and two audio tapes. That is all I have to say.'

Dunlop watched the flickering on the screen for a few minutes before hitting the STOP button on the remote control. He rewound the tape and hooked up the second VCR with a blank tape inserted and two others ready to hand to make copies. He listened to the audio tapes—conversations over the telephone and face to face between Scanlon and the other policemen—as he leafed through the documents. The revised insurance inspector's report was clear enough but the banking records meant little to him. Both Loomis and McCausland mentioned Kippax. Dunlop photocopied the documents and made copies of the audio tapes, so that he ended up with the originals and two duplicates of each piece of evidence.

'Should do it,' he said. He went into the kitchen and opened a bottle of white wine. He poured a glass, drank it straight off, poured another and took it through to the telephone, where he rang Keith Krabbe.

'Got it. It was on the boat. The lot. The man's finished.'

'Good. I've been doing some digging. Not much doubt about it. They rented a car. The girl identified Phil. Fuck, I want Edgar Georges.'

'I'll get him if I can,' Dunlop said. 'Can you back me up on Kippax? You must have something on him.'

There was a pause and Dunlop thought he could hear Krabbe sobbing through a string of high-pitched obscenities. Then the policeman coughed and the grit was back in his voice. 'Yeah. I've got a few things I can say. You going to the SCCA?'

'That's right. Thanks, Keith, and for what it's worth, I'm sorry.'

Krabbe hung up and Dunlop slowly drank his wine as he leafed through the business paper.

Dunlop sat quietly in the conference room of the WPU building in Redfern. Burton had finally shuffled enough paper, made enough notes, sipped enough water. 'Thomas Kippax has been arrested,' he said.

Dunlop said, 'Good.'

'Loomis too, McCausland would have been, but he's hospitalised with only weeks to live, perhaps less.'

204

'That's good too. What about Edgar Georges?'

'Extradition procedures under way. Could be tricky and protracted. He might be more meat for the SCCA. Keith Krabbe's levelled some extraordinary accusations against him.'

'True, every one—bet on it.'

'But you're going to be the main witness against Kippax. He got bail of course. The lawyers are going to string it out to hell and gone. It's going to take a lot of time and you're going to need our services, our protection, Lucas.'

Dunlop leaned back in his chair and thought about the last few years of his life, spent in the service of the WPU. The name change, the people he'd steered to survival and the casualties. He thought about Cassie May Loew and the man he'd killed to get her. And how she'd slipped away. He thought about Ava Belfante and Ann Torrielli and Roy Waterford who dressed as a woman and was as brave as any man he had ever met. He thought about his two brief intimacies with Maddy Hardy, both aborted by 'the job'. And it seemed to him that the world of identity change, re-documentation and relocation was as false and dangerous as the world people called real.

'My name's Frank Carter,' he said. 'And I think I'll take my chances.'

Peter Corris
Set Up

They married in gaol. Cassie May, TV star, and Kerry
Douglas Loew, celebrated prison escapee and armed
hold-up merchant. Cassie is all Loew's ever wanted —
but he's never seen her without the suffocating
company of prison guards and cell walls. He's got ten
years left to serve of a twenty-year sentence. He'll do
anything to get out.

Loew makes a deal with the police. He turns informer
in exchange for the promise of a new name, a new
job, and a new life in a new town.

Ex-cop Luke Dunlop is the Witness Protection Officer
assigned to Kerry Loew. Dunlop knows that in the
code of the underworld, an informer is a dog. A dog
can expect no mercy from his former mates. Especially
if they're on trial for the murder of an assistant police
commissioner.

Loew's enemies are out to get him. Any way they can.
Dunlop's job is to make sure they can't get near him.

Finding a way to hide a man married to a TV star is a
big enough problem for Luke Dunlop. But then he
meets Mrs Cassie May Loew and suddenly he doesn't
care what happens to her husband...

Peter Corris
Cross Off

It's not easy making people disappear, but if Luke Dunlop screws up, someone dies. In Witness Protection there's no margin for error... Every case is a matter of life and death.

Ava Belfante just wants to have fun. She's sexy and flashy and she's got a taste for the good life. She's also got a couple of contracts out on her...

Ava Belfante is trouble waiting to happen. And Luke Dunlop knows it. All he has to do is stop trouble from happening to her first.

'A one-sit adrenalin rush, one of his best.'
GRAEME BLUNDELL ON *SET UP*,
IN *THE AUSTRALIAN*

Paul Mann
Season of the Monsoon

*'I've seen crimes of passion. I've seen
dismemberment, decapitation and sexual mutilation
before. But not like this. Not with this kind of ... wilful
savagery ... This is obscene — this was done by
somebody who enjoys killing.'*

The body of a young actor is pulled out of a lake near
Bombay's Film City. Before dying, he had been
hideously mutilated. Beyond recognition. Beyond
belief.

When another mutilated corpse is found, Inspector
George Sansi must face the unspeakable truth. A
serial killer is loose. A psychopath who kills at
random ... and for pleasure. The only thing Sansi is
certain of is that the killer is a white man. And that he
will kill again.

Racing desperately against time, Sansi finds a clue in
the past ... and uncovers a trail of gruesome murder
that began over half a century before — a trail still
warm with the blood of countless victims. But how
could a murderer return from the past to begin killing
all over again?